D0776644

ve Yourself

a Fright

OTHER YEARLING BOOKS YOU WILL ENJOY:

THE WOLVES OF WILLOUGHBY CHASE, *Joan Aiken*
IS UNDERGROUND, *Joan Aiken*
A CREEPY COMPANY, *Joan Aiken*
BLOSSOM CULP AND THE SLEEP OF DEATH, *Richard Peck*
THE DREADFUL FUTURE OF BLOSSOM CULP, *Richard Peck*
THE GHOST BELONGED TO ME, *Richard Peck*
GHOSTS I HAVE BEEN, *Richard Peck*
VOICES AFTER MIDNIGHT, *Richard Peck*
ISLAND OF THE BLUE DOLPHINS, *Scott O'Dell*
ZIA, *Scott O'Dell*

YEARLING BOOKS are designed especially to entertain and enlighten young people. Patricia Reilly Giff, consultant to this series, received a bachelor's degree from Marymount College and a master's degree in history from St. John's University. She holds a Professional Diploma in Reading and a Doctorate of Humane Letters from Hofstra University. She was a teacher and reading consultant for many years, and is the author of numerous books for young readers.

For a complete listing of all Yearling titles, write to
Dell Readers Service,
P.O. Box 1045,
South Holland, IL 60473.

Books by *JOAN AIKEN*

Juveniles

Give Yourself a Fright

Thirteen Tales of the Supernatural
JOAN AIKEN

A YEARLING BOOK

Published by
Bantam Doubleday Dell Books for Young Readers
a division of
Bantam Doubleday Dell Publishing Group, Inc.
1540 Broadway
New York, New York 10036

The following short stories appearing in this edition were first published
in Great Britain:

For Kitty

and Leslie Norris

Contents

Wing Quack Flap

"It really *can't* be a healthy situation," repeated the welfare officer nervously. Her name was Miss Wenban; she was thin and pretty, with curly dark hair and a pink-and-white complexion; she came from the south and had not yet grown accustomed to tough northern ways and the bleakness of northern landscapes.

"Healthy? Fadge! It's healthy enow!" snarled Grandfather.

Every utterance of Grandfather's came out as a snarl, partly because of the shape of his mouth, which was wide and thin like the slot in a money box; it seemed meant for putting things in, not for words coming out. And indeed, while Grandfather ate his meals, grimly and speedily shoveling in hot-pot, oatcakes, porridge, or kippers, he always insisted on silence.

"Eat your vittles and shurrup, boy! Mealtimes is meant for eating, not for gabbing. Hold your tongue and gan on with your grub."

Pat, whose father had been Irish and talkative, could remember mealtimes at home in Manchester when the

1

three of them, he and Da and Ma, had had so much to say to one another, arguing and joking and laughing, that the food had grown cold on their plates; and not because it was tasteless food either; Ma had been a prime cook; but that was long ago now.

Years ago it seemed, and was; three whole years.

Not that Aunt Lucy wasn't a good cook too. Ma's only sister: it would be funny if she weren't. Ma had been little and pretty and round, like a bird; Aunt Lucy wasn't very like her in other ways. But she really seemed to put her soul into her cooking, Pat thought; that, and trying to keep the cottage as tidy and clean as circumstances would allow. Aunt Lucy's soul didn't seem to come out in anything else she did: wan, silent, and bedraggled, small and gray as the ghost of an otter, with bulging bloodshot scared eyes and flat, scraped-back hair, she crept about the house in a faded cotton overall and fabric slippers with the toes gone out of them. She winced nervously at Grandfather's thumps and shouts, although she had lived with them forty-eight years; and, as long as Grandfather was in the house, she spoke as seldom as possible.

Once, unexpectedly, she had said to Pat, "I can remember when cowslips grew on Kelloe Bank."

"And what if you can?" snarled Grandfather. "What's so remarkable about *that*? You going to sit down and write a letter to the *Northern Echo* about that?"

Aunt Lucy winced and trembled, sank her thin neck down between her shoulders, and went back to separating currants for lardy cake. She had never been able to master reading and writing; it was a sensitive point with her, and Grandfather often referred to her disability, using it as a punishment, either for her or for Pat, whichever of them at that moment had exasperated him. If Pat had a bad report from school—which, luckily, was rare—or did something that annoyed Grandfather—which was much more likely to happen—Aunt Lucy was the one who always came in for the first blast of his ire.

"Hah! I can see you're going to grow up like your daft aunt there. No use to man or beast. Two of ye; what a prospect. Thank the Lord *I* shan't be around to have the job of looking after ye. Thank the Lord I'll be underground."

However, it didn't seem probable that Grandfather would be underground for a long time yet; not long past his mid-sixties, he was hale and stringy as an old root. His coarse white hair stood up on end, thick as marsh grass; out of his red, wind-chapped face—which was only shaved twice a week, sprouted over with grizzled black-and-white stubble the rest of the time—glared two small angry pale-gray eyes, always on the lookout for trouble. Grandfather was in a rage about having been compulsorily retired from his job in the Council Roads Department; he was in a rage about the death of his daughter Sue, Pat's mother, and her husband Micky, in a flu epidemic; he was in a rage about the price of tobacco, and about Stockton United having been beaten by Middlesborough; the only thing that did not put Grandfather in a rage, oddly enough, was the situation in which he, Aunt Lucy, and young Pat were obliged to live.

This situation was why the welfare officer came calling so often. But Grandfather had taken up a rock-hard position about it, from which he would not be budged.

"No. No. *No!* I don't intend to leave this cottage. I was born here—and so was *my* granddad—and they're not getting me out of here till they carry me feet first.

After that they can do as they damn please—I don't care what they do with the place, they can blow it up if they like."

They would never do that, though. The little house itself was protected by all kinds of acts of Parliament. It was listed and scheduled and selected for preservation because a building had always stood there on that site from way back, mentioned in Domesday Book if not earlier, and also because it was one of the very earliest examples of a weaver's cottage, and still had the loom, on which Grandfather's granda had woven, in the back room. A great nuisance the loom was; Pat often longed to take a hatchet to it. Then he could have had a room of his own, instead of being obliged to sleep on the settee in the front room. Also the back room would have been less noisy, though damper than the front, being built into the side of the hill.

It was the location of the house, Kelloe Bank Cottage it was called, that caused welfare visitors to write pages of notes, and medical officers to make continual reports to health committees.

Kelloe Bank Cottage stood, as its name suggested, halfway up a steep, an almost vertical bank, directly between the concrete legs that carried one monstrous motorway, and looking down at another, which circled the foot of the bank, so that all day, and all night, too, a thundering, grinding, roaring, oil-exuding, dust-hurling torrent of cars, trucks, tankers, and vans poured to and fro, to and fro, above and below.

The welfare visitors and health officers often found it difficult to hear or to make themselves heard above the din of the traffic; they tended to stagger away after their visits shaking with strain, and gulping down headache pills; but Grandfather and Aunt Lucy seemed to have developed an ability to hear normal sounds above the roar of motors, and so, after a year or two, did Pat; but then he began to suffer from a lot of bad sore throats and coughs.

That was why Miss Wenban was here again. Once more she had braved the approach to the cottage, which was not an easy one. You had to leave your car in the rest stop on the south side of the east-west motorway down below, climb over a stile, scramble down the embankment, and then trudge along a nasty squelchy footpath which ran through a tunnel under the motorway; emerging on the northern side, you scrabbled your way up an even steeper track to the cottage, whose tidily kept garden, with rows of leeks and cabbages, hung down before it like a striped apron spread over the hillside. Another path led round the cottage and upward from the rear, right under the massive legs of the north-south motorway, and so on up Kelloe Bank; but you could not get very far that way, for the top of the ridge was ruled across, like the seam on a football, by a tremendous barbed-wire fence and a row of mighty pylons, guarded with DANGER signs; beyond that, the other side of the hill was the property of Kelloe Bank Generating Station, and eight huge cooling-towers stood in a group like giants' pepper pots, blocking the access to the plain.

Aunt Lucy believed the cooling towers leaked electricity.

"You can feel it in the air, often; and you can hear it ticking," she whispered confidentially to Miss Wenban. Grandfather, in a rage with what he called "Women's clack," had gone out, muttering venomous things under his breath, and was hoeing between the rows of vegetables, or Lucy would never have found the courage to speak.

With her trembling little claw hands she took hold of Miss Wenban's arm.

"Sometimes you can hear the air tick, like the sound of a spider making its web; other times it's more like a lark singing, or the hum of a bee. When it ticks, I'm scared to strike a match, in case the spark sets off the whole house."

"It's the exhaust fumes that bother *me*," said Miss Wenban, looking at Aunt Lucy rather hopelessly. Then she nibbled the delicious crumbly, buttery wedge of parkin, and sipped the hot fresh cup of tea that Aunt Lucy had set by her on a small tin tray painted with lilies-of-the-valley. "I worry about all the carbon monoxide that must be pouring into your lungs—this is no place for you to live."

"Dad won't ever, ever, shift from this cottage," whispered Aunt Lucy. "And I don't see how we could manage without him. He does all the shopping, you see, in Coalshiels; I never go out anymore; I haven't left the house in twenty years."

"Why not?"

"Dad thinks, better not. I might get lost. It's all so different now from when I was a girl."

"I could take you about, Auntie," offered Pat. "Or I could do the shopping, on my way home from school."

The yellow school bus stopped for Pat every morning, pulling into the rest stop, and brought him back at teatime; on the days when he was well enough to go to school.

"Four and a half weeks you've missed this term,

Pat," said Miss Wenban. "That's awful, you know, in a nine-week term; it's half your education gone."

"I'm sorry," croaked Pat, and he was. "It isn't that I don't like school. And I read when I'm at home, books from the school library. It's my bad throats."

"Is it bad now? Open your mouth. Yes, I can see it is."

Miss Wenban was bothered, also, by the fact that Pat could not bring friends home.

"I have friends at school, all right," he assured her. "But their parents won't let them come here. Too dangerous. It'd mean biking along the motorway."

"Nowt to stop 'em coming over the water meadows, the way I go to get the vittles," growled Grandfather, who had been driven back indoors by a heavy shower. You couldn't hear the rain, because of the traffic roar, but you could see rivulets of water making clean lines on the exhaust-grimed windows. "Mind, I'm not complaining," Grandfather added. "Who wants a passel of young 'uns about the place? Not I! *One's* bad enow."

He directed a scowl at Pat, which made Miss Wenban say firmly, "Pat ought to have company. It's not good for a lad always to be with his elders."

Specially when one of them's a bit simple, Pat could see her thinking, though she was too tactful to say it.

In Pat's view Aunt Lucy was not daft. Just scared off balance by Grandfather, was the conclusion he had come to: otherwise she was sensible enough, when you got her on her own. If it weren't for the horribleness of Da and Ma dying, Pat often thought it was a lucky thing for Aunt Lucy that he had come to live at Kelloe Bank Cottage; since his arrival she had brightened up a bit, and they had tiny secrets together when Grandfather

7

was out of the way, over swallows' nests and butterflies and things Pat told her about school.

"I suppose you can't have radio or TV here under the viaduct—" went on Miss Wenban.

"Who wants that trash? Pack o' rubbish!" snorted Grandfather.

"—but if Pat could keep a pet, now? A—kitten or a parakeet?"

"And isn't *that* just like women's fimble-famble?" burst out Grandfather with utter scorn. "Why would giving the boy a *kitten* cure his sore throat? Any road, I won't have a bird twitterin' and messin' about the house. That I tell you straight! Nor a cat either."

Pat said nothing. He had once *had* a kitten, a little black-and-white cat named Whisky, brought with him when he came to Kelloe Bank Cottage from Manchester. Grandfather had thrown Whisky out, one rainy night, in order to punish Pat for what he called "sulks and whinges"; Pat still held his mind well away from the memory of Whisky's end, flattened under the wheels of a gasoline tanker.

"Just the same, you should have something. What kind of a pet could you keep here? Perhaps a goldfish?"

Miss Wenban was not going to let Grandfather put her down.

"I don't think I'd want a goldfish, thank you," croaked Pat politely.

"Oh. Um." Miss Wenban was momentarily at a standstill. "Well, I shall think about it and come up with some other suggestions next week." And she left before Grandfather could sneer or snarl any more, edging her way through heavy rain down the steep track. Pat watched her with concern through the rain-washed window; he liked Miss Wenban and understood that she meant kindly by him and Aunt Lucy, though her visits tended to bring them much more trouble than if she had stayed away.

"Nearly went tail over tip *that* time," commented Grandfather, watching with a sour grin as the welfare visitor slid and just managed to recover her balance. "It'd be a right laugh if she slipped down the bank and went under a truck. Mayhap then the rest of 'em wouldn't be so keen to come pestering us, nosy-parkering in what's none o' their ruddy business. And as for *you* —*you* just lick her boots!" he grated out, rounding on Lucy. "Wha'd'you want to go feeding her tea an' parkin for? Who told you to do that?"

Poor Lucy started with terror and dropped a plate on the stone floor. Luckily it was only an enamel plate, but a chip flew off and Grandfather stormed at her.

"Now look what you've done! Blubberfingers!"

Fortunately at that moment he noticed that the rain had eased off, and so he went out to resume his garden work.

Lucy rubbed her thumb over the chipped enamel, sucked in her breath, and gave Pat a nervous fluttering smile. She had gone red and white in patches, all over her face, as she mostly did when Grandfather shouted at her.

"Never mind, Aunt Lucy," Pat comforted her. "April's nearly here. Soon Grandfather will be out of doors most of the day. And your chilblains will get better. And my sore throats usually stop in April. Let's have a nibble of parkin," he went on, trying to cheer her, though he found it hard to swallow. "It's grand—the best you ever made."

9

But Aunt Lucy was struggling to say something.

"A pet—Miss Wenban—she says you ought to have a pet."

"Nah," Pat told her quickly. "I don't *want* a pet. It—it just wouldn't do here—not with Grandfather and all."

Aunt Lucy nodded a great many times, very rapidly, with fluttering eyelids.

"When I was a gal—had a collie dog—Lassie," she whispered presently. "Your Uncle Frank—got her for me—time he went to sea."

Pat nodded. Letters from Uncle Frank arrived from places like Hong Kong and Sydney and Recife and Bombay; Uncle Frank, in the merchant navy, was a great traveler. And sounded a kind man.

"Your granda—never did like Lassie," Aunt Lucy whispered. "Didn't like her at all." Pat nodded again. He could easily guess the kind of thing that had happened to Lassie. He put an arm round Aunt Lucy and hugged her.

"Never mind, Auntie! Who wants an old pet that's always needing its water changed, or its litter box emptied?"

Then Aunt Lucy surprised him.

"Got a pet! You—you can share her."

"*You've* got a pet, Aunt Lucy?"

Pat stared around the familiar little front room in bewilderment. Was Aunt Lucy really a bit daft, a bit touched in her wits? He studied the grimy windows, the lace curtains that Aunt Lucy did her best to keep clean, the grubby red inner curtains, the shabby settee, the table with red chenille cloth matching the curtains, three wooden chairs, dresser with plates and pots, mantelshelf with clock and matches, fireplace with built-in oven; on the walls, two pictures of the sea and a calendar with a windmill; on the high shelf a luster cup ("A Present from Scarborough") and a Chinese teapot, a present from Uncle Frank. Twice he let his eyes roam all round the room. Upstairs Aunt Lucy's room contained no more than bed, chair, clothes hook on the back of the door, and window. Well, he decided, it's just a bit of her fancy, like the electricity leaking from the cooling towers. I won't fuss her about it.

Aloud he said, "Can I have a bit more hot in this cup, Aunt Lucy? I let it get cold while Miss Wenban was here."

She poured him half a cupful from the old brown pot; it was still hot, and he drank it in slow, careful sips, letting it slide gently down his sore throat. Doing so, he allowed his eyes to slip out of focus, so that he was able to see two blue teacups and three brown segments of tea, two pointing to right and left, a joined one meeting in the middle of his nose.

"Chinese duck's my pet!" whispered Aunt Lucy, with a triumphant smile. Her face for a moment was quite bright and lively, reminding him of Ma. But don't think of Ma, don't, don't, don't. Aunt Lucy went on, "I keep her in Uncle Frank's teapot. Name's Wing Quack Flap." She nodded and smiled and said again, "You can share her."

Pat nearly choked on his tea. Gulping down the last mouthful he set his cup carefully back on the saucer, while his eyes winked back into focus. But—astonishingly—just before they did so, he could have sworn that he saw a beautiful shining duck, a mandarin duck, fly across the room. The duck was transparent, ghostly, it was like the double images that he had seen when his

11

eyes were out of focus. Through its colors he could see the brown pattern of the wallpaper behind. But the colors were brilliant—red, pink, snowy white, deep blue, dark, lustrous green. The duck circled the room once, at speed, then vanished inside Uncle Frank's Chinese teapot—which was far, far too small to contain the bird that had flown into it. There could not possibly have been enough room inside. Besides, the lid was on.

I'm going barmy too, Pat thought. Head aches. Better take an aspirin.

"Wing Quack Flap," whispered Aunt Lucy again, with that quick, twitching smile, her bulgy eyes flitting toward the window, outside which Grandfather could be heard digging and grunting. Then she took the brown teapot to empty the swillings outside.

While she was out, Pat climbed on one of the chairs, lifted down the Chinese teapot, and looked inside. As he had expected, there was nothing. He carefully put it back, and then, somehow he must have slipped, for the next thing he knew was that he was lying on the floor, and Aunt Lucy was clucking and exclaiming over him.

"I feel a bit queer, Aunt Lucy," he croaked. . . .

The fact that Pat was tucked up on the sofa having flu made no difference at all to the habits of Grandfather, who stomped in and out as usual, gnashing and growling. But fortunately the weather had taken a turn for the better, and at this season Grandfather was a dedicated gardener; he was out of the house more than he was indoors, hoeing, trenching, sowing, transplanting, and mulching all day, while the traffic boomed and howled and fumed above and below him.

Wing Quack Flap

Pat could have his flu in peace, with Aunt Lucy and Wing Quack Flap to keep him company.

Aunt Lucy brewed innumerable hot drinks, which were all that Pat could keep down; Wing Quack Flap soared and swooped overhead, keeping him endlessly amused with her effortless aerobatics. Ninety percent of the time she was airborne; she hardly ever alighted. Sometimes she flew through into the back room, if the door was open, and perched on the loom. Just occasionally she would come to rest on the red chenille tablecloth. When she did come to a stop, what charmed Pat even more than her brilliant colors was her friendly good-humored expression. She was a little like Ma— always looked as if she were just about to break into a laugh. Very different from Grandfather! Her rosy bill curved in a permanent smile, her orange webbed feet turned out at a carefree angle, her black eyes twinkled with humor and knowingness. She shone in the dark little house where, despite Aunt Lucy's best efforts, everything was worn, everything was grimy and shabby from the exhaust fumes and dust that poured round the window frames and under the door and through the curtains. But Wing Quack Flap was not grimy: she was shining and glossy like a new horse-chestnut just popped from its rind.

For the first day or two she was silent; but as Pat's flu took hold of him she began to quack: at the start a comfortable contented gobbling noise, of the kind that ducks make when they are dabbling with their bills through muddy, weedy water: griddle graddle, griddle graddle, griddle graddle. Then, by and by, as she flew, she brought out a loud joyful honking quack: WAAARK, wark-wark-wark-wark-wark. Pat could hear it easily above the sound of the traffic, and he thought it quite the nicest noise he had heard since the days when his father used to sing "Peg in a Low-Backed Car" and other Irish songs. Often Pat fell asleep to the sound of Wing Quack Flap's conversation.

"But, Aunt Lucy—is it right to keep her in the teapot?" he muttered one day, between temperatures, when Grandfather was out doing the shopping at Coalshiels Co-op. "The pot's too small for her."

"Nowhere else to put her. Nowhere that's safe," said Aunt Lucy.

There came a day when Pat's flu rose up like a river in spate and nearly swamped him entirely; when light and dark fled past one another in a flickering, speeding race like the headlights of the traffic along the two motorways; when Pat's thumping heart and his drawing, dragging breath made such a deal of noise that he was unable to hear the trucks and tankers above and below; when Dr. Dilip Rao came from Coalshiels, and a nurse in dark blue and brass buttons from Hutton End; when there was talk about an ambulance and hospital; only, they were saying to each other, how could they manage to carry a stretcher up the steep slippery path, let alone through the narrow tunnel under the Hawtonstall Highway?

In the middle of their argument Pat sat up in bed, watching the zigzags of Wing Quack Flap, who was in the back room playing follow-my-leader with herself in and out of Great-Grandfather's loom.

"I'd rather stay at home," he announced. "I'd rather stay with Aunt Lucy and Wing Quack Flap."

No one paid any heed to his actual words: they were

all so startled to see him sit up and act like a human being.

"Peck o' silly chatteration, talk o' fetching the boy to hospital," growled Grandfather, stumping in out of the garden. "Nowt ails the lad but a touch o' grippe; and that's on its way out. Young 'uns weren't mollycoddled in hospitals when *I* were a lad; you stayed home an' got better by yoursen." He scowled at Dr. Dilip.

"Well," said the doctor, "in view of the difficulty with the ambulance . . ." He glanced at Nurse Enderby.

"I'll come in again this afternoon," she promised. "And first thing tomorrow."

Aunt Lucy said nothing at all but looked nervously from one to the other. While the doctor examined Pat, she had taken Nurse Enderby into the back room and held a conversation with her, pressed up against the loom. Now Lucy was kneading and wringing her hands as if she rolled a strip of lardy-cake dough on a floured board. And if anyone had stood close beside her, they might have heard her whisper, "It isn't right, it isn't right, it isn't right!"

Dr. Dilip and Nurse Enderby left, and Pat let himself slip down under the covers again. He felt tired and giddy from so much company.

"I'll make that call for you," murmured the nurse to Aunt Lucy on her way out. Luckily Grandfather did not hear.

"Beef tea—put on a kettle—make a cup of hot—" fluttered Aunt Lucy, and took the brown jug from the dresser and went out to the tap at the side of the cottage.

"Now those daft poke-noses have left," snarled Grandfather, suddenly rounding with unexpected savagery on Pat as he lay limp under the blanket of knitted

15

squares—"now *they're* out of the road, what was that I heard you say about your Aunt Lucy and some rubbish?"

Pat felt weak and hopeless. He could not protect himself from Grandfather's little gray gimlet eyes, which bored into Pat like laser beams, and his grating, angry voice which demanded again, "What was that I heard you say? Quack quack flip flap—or something daft?"

"Wing Quack Flap is *not* daft!" feverishly flung back Pat. "She's not daft—she's our duck—our beautiful duck —and she lives in the Chinese teapot—"

"*What* did you say? I'll give you a Chinese teapot, my lad!" roared Grandfather. "I'm not having *you* grow up ninepence-in-the-shilling, like your sawney aunt! I'm stopping any such nonsense *now*— once and for all. Wing Quack Flap, indeed! I twisted *that* perishing bird's neck twenty years ago, and all! I'll have no more of it now!"

And he strode across to where he could reach the high shelf, stretched up, and seized hold of the Chinese teapot.

"Wait, you, till I get this window open—Wing Quack Flap, indeed!"

"Grandfather, *no!*" cried Pat in agony.

But Grandfather, with a great swing back of his arm, hurled the teapot out through the open window—flung it so hard and savagely that Pat, waiting for the crash against the garden wall, heard, instead, a shriek of brakes down below on the motorway, and then the tinkle of smashed glass, and shouts, and horns blaring.

"What in the *world* is going on in here?" demanded Miss Wenban the welfare visitor, walking into the room just at that moment.

*   *   *

Grandfather had been taken down to the police station to be charged. Not with manslaughter—mercifully for him, in the pileup caused when the teapot he had thrown out went through the windshield of an articulated car-transporter, although numerous people were hurt, and thousands of pounds' worth of damage had been done, nobody had actually died. But when the police came up to the cottage Grandfather had flown into such a passion and resisted arrest so ferociously that he was now in a cell and would probably remain there for some days. But that was all right, for Uncle Frank was flying home from Naples, where Nurse Enderby had managed to contact him by radio telephone.

"He says he was thinking of retiring this year in any case," Nurse Enderby told Aunt Lucy and Pat. "Thank you, Miss Blackhall, I wouldn't say no to another cup of your tea, and a sliver of that lardy cake. Your brother said he had it in mind to start a little baker's shop, in Tunstall, and maybe you and the boy could live with him there."

"Then Granda can stay here on his own," said Pat, comfortably leaning back on his sagging heap of cushions. "He'll like that better than having us."

Aunt Lucy nodded several times without speaking. But her eyes shone brighter than they had for months.

After Nurse Enderby had gone Pat said sadly, "I'm sorry—I'm very sorry about—about your teapot, Aunt Lucy. It was all my fault. I shouldn't have said anything to Grandfather. And I'm sorry about—"

The name stuck in his throat. Already he was beginning to wonder if Wing Quack Flap had existed at all, in any way—or had she simply been part of his illness? Had he made up the whole thing?

But Aunt Lucy, nodding over and over, wide eyed, solemn, patted his hand several times and whispered, "Never mind, never mind! Can't be helped. Besides— you were right. Teapot not big enough. No! But listen now—listen!"

Shaking her head, muttering scoldingly to herself, she pattered away to the window and opened it wide. "Not too cold now. Listen!" she said again. "Listen, Pat!"

Outside, April twilight was thickening, and though the traffic roar could still be heard, at this time of the evening the noise had diminished a little; indeed, as Aunt Lucy stood by the casement, her finger conspiratorially to her lips, a brief lull came, in which no vehicle passed on either highway, above or below.

And during that lull something else could be heard instead: a loud series of triumphant honking quacks: WAARK, WAARK, WAARK, wark-wark-wark-wark- wark. Round and round the house the cry circled, three, four, five, six times; then, fading away, it receded into the far distance.

Back to China, perhaps, thought Pat.

Soon the traffic roar began again.

The Old Poet

I had to fly to England for college interviews, and was going to stay there at least a month. My mother said: "Very good, my boy, you can go to your great-grandfather's funeral and represent this bit of the family."

"His funeral? But he's still alive."

"But Posy writes (Posy! What a name!) that the doctors don't give him more than three weeks at the outside. Well, it will be a release for her; heaven knows she has nursed him devotedly. I hope she is well rewarded for her trouble."

"Is he rich?"

"There must be a steady income from all those *Collected Poems* and *Selected Poems* and revised *Collected Poems*—and the verse dramas, they do those on the radio, I believe—"

My great-grandfather, William Beaumaris, aged ninety-eight, had three times declined the honor of becoming poet laureate. Didn't fancy having to cough up poetry to order, he said. Sooner write advertising copy about women's underwear. Which he had done at one time, to support his muse. Posy was his fourth wife.

I had never met my great-grandfather because we lived in Kenya. And also because my mother had had a mortal row with him over the way he treated *her* mother. "As an unpaid secretary. Women were only intended as *vessels,* according to him." But that was all over forty years ago, and I certainly had a curiosity to meet this grand, mysterious old man, who had been at Queen Victoria's funeral, and sat on Gladstone's knee, and known George Bernard Shaw, and went on a trip to Finland with Bertrand Russell. And had written more sonnets than Shakespeare, more lyrics than Herrick, more long, obscure dramatic poems than Browning. Most of these I had not read.

I did read the lyrics, on the plane, going to Heathrow. They were very lyrical but quite dry—half Coke, half lemon.

> The love I chased has turned to laurel
> and now repels my rash embrace
> armored in leather leaves, her branches
> tough, brittle, sharp, and lacking grace;
>
> come autumn, when the molten forest
> shrieks at the gale with which it strives
> she stands, smug, safe, and wholly proper
> as guardian of suburban drives.

I never got around to the sonnets and the verse dramas; or, at least, not then.

When they asked, after my college interviews, where they should send the news of acceptance or rejec-

tion, I gave Great-Grandpapa's address—that created a
startled and respectful silence each time—then I caught
a train to Scotland, which was where he now lived,
though he was not of Scottish origin; our ancestors were
a Norman hanger-on of William I, and a Welsh princess
called Nesta.

I had tried to telephone Posy, but could not get
through; and Mother's letter had not received an answer, or not before I left home, so I had no idea what to
expect, or even if *I* was expected. The last part of the
journey entailed a bus journey over quite a large piece
of Scotland, and then I found myself on the wrong side
of a loch.

"Mr. Beaumaris's place?" someone said. "Over
there"—and jerked a thumb.

Half a mile away, over the water, among a great
wedge of forest, I could make out the shape of gray
buildings.

By this time I was nearly out of cash. With my last
five-pound note I paid a local to take me across in his
boat.

"Ye'll know Mr. Beaumaris?" he said skeptically.
"There's a wheen newspaper folk try to interview him,
whiles." His tone suggested that they never succeeded.

"I'm his great-grandson."

"Ay, is that a fact?" His tone was no less skeptical
than before.

When he dropped me on a small granite pier I had
half a mind to ask him to ferry me back again; suppose I
found myself marooned in this tree-darkened spot (for
the forest came right down to the edge of the water)?
Suppose Great-Grandpapa had died while I was making
my way to him? But I hadn't enough money to pay for

the return ride, so thanked the boatman, hoisted my pack, and set off through trees to the dimly glimpsed mansion.

As I drew nearer I could hear the sound of a chain saw: a malevolent, high-pitched shriek. The sound was ominous in those terribly silent woods. The trees were enormous. Under them grew a little grass, thin and moss-infested, like the sparse dandruffy hairs on an old man's head. There was a kind of path, and then a small-ish open space. Beyond it I could see a side of the house, with a terrace and a row of windows; opposite the house lay the shore of the loch, which curved round here in a small bay. On the rocky shoreline grew a huge tree: it spread out like a hand, not a single trunk but about six of them, gray and smooth fingers reaching upward. At the foot of this tree stood a tractor, and up in the boughs were a couple of men, swinging themselves about, agile as monkeys, lopping off smaller branches. I thought they were amazingly carefree considering how high up they were—at least forty feet aboveground—until, coming closer, I saw they wore crash helmets and were secured with safety harness which they had made fast to the main boles.

I was so absorbed in watching their operation that I did not, until I was quite close to him, see the man lying on the quilted lounger, observing the men with an ex-pression of deep hostility.

"And who the devil are *you*?" he snarled at me.

There was no mistaking who *he* was. I had seen that gaunt old face, that thin-lipped mouth and cockatoo-crest of white hair on plenty of book jackets and color-supplement pages. He was wrapped in a tartan rug and leaned against a pile of pillows; but he did not, to my eye, look as if he were within three weeks of death; far from it.

"I'm your great-grandson," I said. "William Malkin."

"And who, pray, gave you leave to come here?"

"Mother did write—to Posy—"

"Posy!" he growled, without troubling to pursue my story further. "Look what she's seen fit to have done. Do you know where we *are*, here? This is one of the last stands of true Caledonian forest—and *she* has to send for men in crash helmets to spay that ash tree—a rowan, mark you, a mountain ash, magic tree, Thor's own tree —they are lopping it, they are crippling it, and they are whittling it down to little more than a stump. Not only that, but they intend to tether the boughs together in some damned spiderweb of steel chains—garrrrhhh!"

His growl was ferocious.

I said, "Why are they doing that, Great-Grandfather?"

"Delilah!" he muttered. "How does she know my heart is not in that tree? Or perhaps she does!"

"Perhaps the tree needs the treatment?" I suggested doubtfully.

One of the workmen, passing by, agreed with me. "Aye," he said in a scolding tone, "aye, man, ye should not have allowed that tree to grow in that gait; ye should not have allowed it in the first place!"

"I did not happen to be *here*, a hundred years ago, when that tree first sprouted!" my grandfather hurled after him. Then he muttered to himself, "I daresay the fellow thinks I was here then. But I'll put a curse on them, I'll put a curse on the lot of them, so I will!"

"Are you able to put curses on people, Great-Grandfather?"

23

It seemed not at all improbable; he looked as if he had plenty of that kind of power in him. When he turned his blazing eyes on me I took a step backward.

"Have I the power to curse? Of course I have! Ninety-three years of poetry—doesn't that add up to power? What happens to a gas when you compress it? What do you get? An explosion. Cool down air until it turns liquid—you could boil a pint of it on a lump of ice."

"Have you cursed many people, then?"

"I'll tell you three I did curse," he said venomously. "Arnwit, Thoroughgood, and Threlkeld. Withered them up like raffia."

"But why? Why did you? Because they were bad poets?"

James Arnwit, Jasper Thoroughgood, and Morton Threlkeld had been the poets who accepted the laureateship when Beaumaris refused it. Arnwit and Thoroughgood had died, respectively of a stroke and falling under a bus; Threlkeld was fast approaching his end from alcoholism.

"Bad poets," he muttered. "Of course they are bad poets. And to have *them*— each in turn—offered the job when *I* was passed over—"

"But—good heavens—I thought it was the other way round. But why? You are a much better poet," I said in true family fervor.

With low-voiced hissing fury he told me why he had been repeatedly snubbed by the government. It was because of something he had done at Queen Victoria's funeral—*what,* I could not quite gather; unfortunately the chain saw gave a particularly virulent screech just then. Perhaps he spat at the coffin? Shouted a rude word or threw an egg? He would have been about fifteen at the time, an age when good manners have flown away on the breeze. Anyway, whatever it was, his action had deprived him of the laureateship. And he was still in a rage about it.

"I'll curse them, I'll keep cursing them," he mumbled. And seemed gathering himself up to do so, when, nervously looking away from him, I saw a stunningly pretty girl approaching. Surely this could not be Posy? She looked no more than seventeen, blond, with perfect features and huge gray-green eyes.

"Now *don't* get angry, don't," she wheedled, dropping down on her knees by his chair and placing a soothing hand over both of his as they knotted and unknotted themselves on the tartan blanket. "It wastes your time, it wastes your power. Who's this?" and she turned the great eyes on me, inquiring, wondering, just a little calculating.

"It's my great-grandson," growled the old boy. He had never questioned my credentials; but it is true that I do look very like my mother, and she like hers.

"I am Meridian Jones," the girl informed me as if the name ought to be familiar. Another poet? And she added proudly, "I am William's acolyte."

I knew he had always had some teenage admirer fluttering around him wherever he was; it was to them that the lyrics were addressed. My mother often said she wondered how Posy stood them,around the place; but she added, "I supposed they make themselves useful carrying trays and doing the dusting." This one didn't look like the sort to do any dusting; but she had brought a mug of malted milk out on a silver tray. Beaumaris swigged it down while Meridian Jones watched him worshipfully. Then she ran her fingers through his thick white hair, and said, "Now, don't think ugly thoughts about the tree men; don't! They have to do their job. Make up a poem, why don't you, and I'll write it down. Make up a nice poem to me." She pulled a notebook from her jeans pocket.

"I've written too bloody many poems. Poetry sucks the life out of you. It's like a fungus. I'd sooner curse somebody," he said fretfully. His angry eyes flicked about the clearing, and came to rest on me. I felt like the young lady of Smyrna in Lear's limerick "who seized on the cat and said, 'Granny, burn that!'" I had not the least wish to fall under a curse just before going up to university.

At this moment a woman came round the corner of the house who must, of course, be Posy. She was in her mid-thirties, plump and smiling, with a serene, lived-in face and kind brown eyes.

"I was wondering when you'd turn up," she said to me. "You are William Malkin, aren't you? Did you get into your university?"

"What university?" grumbled the old man. "Why do you want to go to a university? *I* never went to university. Didn't need to."

"I shan't know for a week or two," I told Posy.

"You'll stay here till then, of course. We'll be glad to have you—shan't we, Meridian?"

The younger girl gave me an admiring look.

At that moment the men in the tree began their netting operation, slinging a steel cable from bole to bole, fastening it with huge screws which they plunged deep into the timber. The old man winced as each screw went in.

"Murderers! Torturers! Tying up the tree in a bloody spiderweb."

"Darling Will, it has to be done. Or, next winter, the tree will blow down. It is done for the tree's own good. That's a sick tree you have there."

"What's the use of being protected if you're half dead already?" demanded Beaumaris.

Meridian looked my way again, giving me a very sweet and slightly knowing smile, as if she enlisted me on the side of youth against the silly older generation. I noticed my great-grandfather notice this, and he did not like it. I thought he did not want his disciple making eyes at young men.

Now the workmen came down the tree, hitched their tractor onto a truck which had already been filled with the piled debris of cut-off branches, and drove briskly away over the grass, touching their crash helmets respectfully to Posy and my great-grandfather as they passed by.

Beaumaris was speaking as the tractor trundled off, but the noise it made drowned his words. He pointed a finger at me in a hortatory manner.

"Now come along, darling," said Posy. "Time for your nap. And you'll have to take it inside, for there's going to be a storm, had you noticed?"

It was true; black clouds were piling up across the sky. Here under the huge trees the sky was only to be seen at all in small patches, but the light was dying fast; although only midafternoon it seemed like late evening.

A low chatter of thunder could be heard from the foot of the loch.

"Once we get a storm here," Posy told me, "it goes

round and round. Trapped by the mountains, don't you see; it can't escape. Come along, Will, my honey."

She helped the old man out of his lounger. Meridian Jones fluttered around, rather unhelpfully, getting in the way and making gestures which came to nothing. Posy was quite capable of helping her husband indoors by herself. At length Meridian followed with the tray and empty mug, leaving me to fold the chair and take it indoors with the rug and cushions.

In the house the old man was muttering about spiderwebs as Posy helped him onto a daybed and made him comfortable in a small room off the huge main hall. "There would be spiderwebs in the glass of the windows; and webs across their eyes; and spider cracks in the glaze of their mirrors."

I could hardly decide if this was a poem or a curse; but the girl Meridian was enthusiastically jotting it down in her notebook, so I assumed that it was a poem.

"You come in here!" the old man called to me through the open doorway. So I walked in nervously, as Posy nodded to me to obey.

"Here." He pulled a ring off his thin middle finger. It was an old-fashioned gold signet with a black stone, jet perhaps, and a crest which seemed to be a spiderweb. "Too late to leave you anything in my will. If that's what you were hoping?" he added in a nasty tone.

"Of course I wasn't!"

"Don't interrupt. You can have this to remember me by."

I didn't think I'd have the least trouble remembering him. Nor did he, for he laughed in a private kind of way, and went on, "It's the best curse of all. Come along: put on the ring."

Under his brilliant eye, what could I do? I slid on the ring—my little finger was the only one it would fit.

"Now *you* have the power," my great-grandfather said. "And much good may it do you. And now leave me in peace."

I went out and closed the door. Posy showed me to a huge damp upstairs bedroom with its own mahogany toilet in a powdering closet. The windows looked out toward the patch of grass and the shoreline where the old man had been sitting. So we had a grandstand view of the pale-purple flash of lightning which, at that moment, came jagging down out of the sky and struck the six-pronged ash tree, winding among the trunks like a bunch of flames in the hand of Jupiter. The tree flamed like an Olympic torch.

"Oh, dear! After all that trouble and money spent," said Posy placidly. "Now, of course, Will is bound to say that putting that steel cable on the tree attracted the lightning. And for all I know he may be right."

Or he could, I thought, say that he had cursed the cable and the gelded tree.

But William said nothing, for he died at the moment when the lightning hit the tree; or at least this was a likely guess, for he was found quietly dead and cold in his bed, a couple of hours later, when Posy took him a cup of tea.

So I went to the funeral. The rude epithet shouted after Queen Victoria must have been overlooked, at last, or put out of mind, for the ceremony took place in the Abbey, with full appropriate splendors, and William was given a place in Poets' Corner. And all the time the service went on, I looked up at the windows and wondered if I could see spiderweb cracks in them.

I was given my place at Oxford, but have derived little benefit from it, for my great-grandfather's curse came into operation almost at once: I began writing poetry, and find I have no time left over for any other activity. Poetry, as he said, sucks the life out of you; it is like a parasitical growth.

And with it comes the power to curse; but I have not used that yet.

Do Not
Alight Here

Fred and I can generally see them when we are together. And, when we are separate, the one of us who has the locket can see them. When we are together we can see all kinds of things—an old ghost-cat who sits, sometimes for days together, on top of the wall that separates our garden from the churchyard, for instance. Why should the ghost of a cat sit on that wall for such long stretches of time? What keeps him there? No one will ever know. When we are together, Fred and I have sometimes called to him, "Hey, Puss, Puss, Puss!" But he never takes any notice. He's watching something too intently. And we see a fisherman casting his line at the end of Hexton Mill Pond, so full of effluent that no fish has swum there in thirty years; and sometimes a shapeless body, you can't tell if it is male or female, can be seen dangling from the crooked oak that leans over Barton Hollow; and once, when we were together, we saw the Messerschmitt that crashed flaming with all its load of bombs into Greystoke Hospital; forty-six years after the event, we saw it.

When we were small, people used to scold us for

being fanciful—"making up stories"; so, ever so long ago, we learned to keep quiet about what we saw.

We are twins, but not identical ones; one of us was born half an hour before the other. In fact we don't resemble each other much at all; people are often quite surprised to learn that we are even brothers. Fred is tall, fair, and gangling; I am short, dark, and wiry. When we were younger we used to fight all the time; Fred was stronger and used to bang my head on the quarry tiles, but I was better at wrestling and soon found out how to do things that would make him bawl with agony. Ma said she didn't dare ever leave us together for more than ten minutes, or she'd come back to find broken glass, torn curtains, and feathers from exploded cushions all over the floor. Let alone blood and teeth.

Of course we don't do that anymore now. We're civilized now. But, for that reason, Ma always refused to tell us which one was the older, which was born first. Right up to the day she died. When she was at her last gasp Fred hung over her in the hospital bed and urged, "Come on, Ma, don't clam up on us *now*!" But she pressed her lips tight together—though she'd been yelling and carrying on about the awful pain in her legs only the moment before—and so she died that way, lips tight shut and eyes glaring at us in fierce refusal.

And it was the same in her will. She'd no money to leave, of course, only the insurance policy she'd always kept paid up, which was pinned to her corsets—"the wealth" she used to call it—which poor sad old Pa drank himself to death on in less than a year after she went. Apart from that, there was a grubby old page torn from a penny notebook which said, *I leave the Caul in which one of my Sons was born to both of them. They'd best*

*take Turns carrying it, and heres Hoping it bring them
the luck it never brought me.*

Ma came from Liverpool, you see, and up there a
caul is thought very lucky. Sailors buy them from hospitals if the mothers of the babies don't want to keep
them. The baby isn't born right inside the caul, of
course; only the head. It's like a bit of membrane; and
ours was shrunk up by now so it was only like a little dark
bit of withered leaf, or cobweb, which Ma had put inside
of an old small dented silver locket, black with tarnish,
fastened to a thin grubby chain; Ma used to wear it
round her neck, but Fred and I just carry it loose in a
pocket. Like I said, we're civilized now, so, as she ordered, we take it in turns, a month each. Unless one of us
happens to need it real bad for some special reason; like
when Fred was trying to raise the cash to buy a flat in
Cascella, for instance, or when my greyhound Sparky
was a favorite at White City. Then we'd try and reach
what they call an agreement. It didn't always work.

That was one reason why I was traveling down to the
airport with Fred. I wanted to try and persuade him to
let me start my turn a few days early.

"It's only a stupid fight," said Fred. "What's it matter
if you win or not? It's only local—in the long run, who
cares?"

"Pearly cares."

"In two years," said Fred, "You'll have forgotten
Pearly's name."

Even if that were true, even if I'd forgotten her in
two months, it made no difference to the way I feel *now,*
I thought; and I said, "Anyway, why do *you* need it so
particular just today? You're only going on a routine hop
to Stockholm."

Fred is an air steward. His height makes the job a bit awkward for him, but the lady passengers love his curly fair hair and honest blue eyes offering them Pepsi or Gin-and-tonic.

"Well I'll tell you," said Fred, after a glance round the carriage, to make sure nobody was within earshot. "It's not such a routine trip. When I come back, I'm planning to bring a little packet with me which ought to pay for a month or two in the sun. I'm just about fed up with rain and fog every day."

And he glanced out irritably at the landscape which, in between our home stop, Blagdon, and the airport stop, gets very ruined looking, with huge acreage of deserted gravel pits, all half full of water, and old quarry sites, and abandoned shunting yards with nothing left in them to shunt, and pylons with power lines going every which way, and derelict industrial buildings, and general mess. I've sometimes thought—this kind of thing is what used to get Fred and me called fanciful—that the landscape looks *angry;* that it really hates us humans for what we've done to it.

In the middle there's this abandoned station called Winterstead, where the trains don't stop anymore; DO NOT ALIGHT HERE it says in big red letters on white signs, two or three of them along each crumbling empty platform, and the station buildings and steps are mostly demolished, just a skeleton left of the glass canopy, and empty gaping ticket office and parcel rooms. Nobody in their senses would *want* to alight there; nobody could, most of the time. For the trains don't stop there anymore but scurry through as if rats were after them.

But it's on Winterstead platform that Fred and I

have one of our regular sightings, if we are together; or, like I said, if the one that's on his own has the locket with him.

It's a mother and child; the mother only a girl, not very old, wearing a skimpy old-fashioned flowered suit, jacket, and long narrow skirt; she sits there as if she's bored nearly to death in a little glass shelter halfway along the long narrow platform, and her kid in a stroller beside her. Plainly she hasn't the least intention of catching a train; probably doesn't have the fare to go anywhere. She's just come up onto the station platform to keep the kid amused watching the trains go by; you can tell she's bored rigid, her mouth half open in one long yawn. And the kid, what you can see of it, just a bit of pale face inside of a lot of wrappings, the kid sitting there, no more lively than a suet dumpling, but still, I suppose, paying attention, looking out sharply enough to see what's going and what's coming. The girl's face is a bit familiar, or seems so, perhaps by now just because we've seen her so often. The first sighting was when we were both about eleven.

How do we know they aren't real people? Why, by the eyes. There's times when the train has crawled slowly by, and we could see them, close as the assistant on the other side of a shop counter; and you can see their eyes are just two holes that go right through—as if they were cutout figures made from paper; through those holes you can get a glimpse of the gray sky, or the bars of the iron fence behind. It's a queer feeling, not at all nice, when sometimes the girl will turn her head and look at you, and those hollow empty circles with nothing in them will focus right on you, or seem to. Still, they don't appear to mean us any particular harm; and have never done me any, or not yet at least. Mind, I've never had the slightest intention of getting off the train at Winterstead. Nobody else seems to see the girl and her kid, only Fred and me. Why do they sit there? Heaven knows. Maybe one day she got so bored she jumped onto the electrified track; or pushed the kid onto it. I've never heard tell. Whatever happened, happened a long time ago; the station at Winterstead has been closed to the public ever since I've been riding that route. And that's a good while now, since Fred went to Godsham High and I went to the Robert Barrington Comprehensive. These days I have a job checking supplies at the airport gift- and newsstands; that was another reason why I was traveling down with Fred; apart from the pleasure of his company.

"Come on—be a sport," I said. "Think of Ma."

"Huh!"

"Well," I reminded him, "you really owe me two days, because of that time you wanted to take out Jodie Faireweather."

"And a right load of sour apples she turned out to be," he said.

Well, we argued it one way and the other until we'd passed through Winterstead station, where, as usual, the mother and child were sitting glumly surveying the track, in spite of a black northeast wind blowing great lumps of half-digested rainy mist across the blasted landscape.

"Maybe they're waiting for somebody that's going to come and rescue them one day," Fred says whimsically.

"Like a knight in shining armor? Don't try to change the subject," I said. "Come on—give. We'll be at the airport in another couple of minutes and you don't want any nosy parker watching the hand-over."

We feel private about our caul.

Rather to my surprise, Fred suddenly did give in.

"Okay, okay—but I want it back Wednesday."

"Wednesday—what if—"

"Never you mind what if," he said. "I want it back Wednesday." And he fished the little dented black oval, that was shiny at the edges with rubbing, out of his uniform pants pocket and passed it over, all warm. Fred wasn't really supposed to change into his uniform till he got to the DAS staff changing rooms at the airport, but he always preferred to change at home because girls on the train used to admire his neat navy-blue with mop of fair curls atop.

I couldn't help being a bit suspicious of this sudden turnaround, and shot him a sharp glance, but he was smiling sweeter than rum-and-coke, so I said, "Thanks, big brother," sweet as he, kept my suss to myself, and stowed the locket away in my own pants pocket.

We got out at the airport stop and rode up on the escalator into the main check-in level. Fred a step behind and below me, but still able to see over my head. The girl in front of me half turned round, noticed him, and gave him a big careful up-and-down; me she hardly noticed.

"Well, ta-ta then, see you Wednesday," said Fred a minute later, when we'd slid along the walkway into the airport concourse, and he was making for the airline staff departure entrance that was marked PRIVATE, STAFF ONLY, NO ADMITTANCE.

"So long, Fred," I said, nodding, and then, as he went through the door, I spun right round and, instead of going along to the gift stall and newsstand that I serviced, I headed back to the station, not on the walkway this time, but running fast, dodging my way like a footballer between the exiting passengers pushing their clumsy luggage trolleys. I flipped out my rail pass at the station ticket barrier and catapulted down the stairs, just in time to throw myself on board a train that was headed back the way we had come. Fred had had about two minutes to discover his loss and come after me—but his check-in time was due and he'd never risk it.

Of course, after that hair's-breadth timing, the wretched train then enraged me by waiting for another three minutes. But Fred didn't show. And in the end it did give an electrical whinny and start moving off back toward Winterstead and Blagdon. Just before it did so, the door opened and an old girl tumbled into my section. She seemed wholly out of breath; and sat herself down opposite me panting hard and, for some reason, giving me very nasty looks. I raised my brows at her a bit, but thought, well, you can't please 'em all.

"I remember *you*," she said suddenly and sharply when she had got her breath back. "You are Stan Sillinge. I used to have you in my current-events class at Barrington."

Then I remembered her too—old Meddlesome Matty, we used to call her. Mitchell-Matthiesson, her real name was. She was the senior mistress my last term at school, then retired to become a magistrate and JP. I bet she gave them a hard time on the bench; she was as tough as an old hockey boot.

"At it again, I see," she said unpleasantly when she'd taken a few more breaths. "You were always a tiresome, sneaky, ill-conditioned boy at school."

"I *beg* your pardon, missis," I said, keeping cool, pretending not to recognize her. "I think you must have mistaken me for someone else."

"No, I haven't," she says. "When we get to the terminus I'm going to hand you over to the police—*I* saw you pick that man's pocket on the walkway."

And without another word she leaned across and suddenly whipped the locket out of my windcheater pocket. "Hmmn, antique silver, probably worth quite a lot."

"*Do* you mind?" I said furiously. "That happens to be my property. The person ahead of me on the walkway was my brother Fred—and he had just picked *my* pocket, coming up the escalator."

I'd felt him—though he'd nicked it as expert as threading silk through a needle—just when the girl turned to look at him. But I'd been on the lookout, all along, for something of the kind.

He'd given in much too easily.

"Your *brother*— I never heard such rubbish," the old girl said. "Why, you aren't anything like each other. He's about twice your height, and fair."

Ma had always made a point of our going to different schools, because we fought so. That's why old Mitching had never seen Fred.

"If he's your brother," she added, "I'm the Princess of Wales."

I was annoyed. "He *is* my brother! and we have this family—er—thing. Token. And we—take turns carrying it. It's a kind of—kind of game," I finished rather lamely.

"A likely story! So," she said with awful sarcasm, "I suppose you expect me to believe that we can now go back to the airport and find your brother, and he will substantiate what you say."

"Of course he would!" (Though privately I wasn't at all sure that, if Fred was in one of his mean moods, he might not deny the whole story, just to put me in an awkward spot.) "Only," I added, "the thing is, he was just going off on a flight to Stockholm. He's an air steward."

"Naturally! Very convenient! And when will he be back?"

"Not till Wednesday afternoon. It was the DAS two-thirty flight. One-night stopover."

"I don't believe you," she said. "Anyway, you may tell your story to the police; they will be able to check if the firm really does employ a brother of yours."

I thought how furious Fred would be to have police conducting inquiries about him at DAS where, up to now, he'd managed to keep his nose clean.

"Why don't you just listen—" I was beginning, but at that moment the train slid to a jerky halt—the kind that usually means fog, or a signal at red, or maintenance men working on the line ahead. Looking out, I was surprised to see that we'd reached Winterstead already; for once we were actually stopped alongside the derelict, weed-grown platform right in front of one of the signs that said DO NOT ALIGHT HERE.

No carriage doors slammed, needless to say. Nobody got out.

But old Meddlesome Matty, looking out the window, gave a kind of gasp.

"What in the *world* does that silly, silly girl think she is doing with that unfortunate child?" says she. "Good heavens—stop, *stop*!"

And without another word to me, she's opened the carriage door and nipped straight out onto the crumbling concrete—leaving the door swinging—and runs back along the platform, out of my view.

And, you can guess what happened next: the train started again, as jerkily as it had stopped, causing the door to swing smartly to and latch itself again.

"Hey, come back!" I was yelling, but my voice was drowned by the clatter of a southbound express that raced through on the other side of the platform, and meanwhile our own train, gathering speed, slid northward on its way to Blagdon.

What could I do? Not a single thing. I sat sweating with rage and helplessness. Pull the cord? There was a hundred-pound fine for misuse, and to tell the truth, I didn't want to tangle any more with old Matty or the police just then. I thought I'd wait a day till Fred was back, then we could look her up in the phone book—she was bound to be there, being a JP and all—and we might go and see her together. No doubt by and by she'd find some way of getting herself off Winterstead station— though it was almighty queer, I thought to myself, that she, too, had seen the ghostly mum and kid. Presumably because she was carrying our locket. Served her right. I wondered what she had seen the mum *doing*— from her behavior it must have been something much more drastic than anything Fred and I had ever witnessed.

Who *did* that girl remind me of?

One of these days I'd remember.

I got myself home, stopping off on the way for some Chinese takeout, called my head office to say I'd a bad cold, but would be back to work tomorrow—which they took pretty ungraciously—then changed into a track suit and phoned Pearly. But Pearly, it seemed, was out. And while I was sitting with one leg hooked over the settee arm, listening to her bell going ring-ring, and then a pause, ring-ring, and then a pause, I had one of those queer I-don't-know-what-you-call-'ems that come over you, sometimes, for no reason, when the whole universe shifts a couple of paces to one side, and you wonder what the hell you are doing, in this small front room in the middle of nowhere, looking at the dusty telephone, and the brown hearthrug, and the neat white carrier-bag of Chinese takeout food steaming on the floor. And who is this *you*, anyway? And how long have you been in that place?

Shaking myself out of this horrible mood—which, thank goodness, never lasts more than a minute or two —I switched on the radio for some music. And, instead, got the announcer's voice saying: "News has just come that a DAS Boeing 727 on a routine flight to Stockholm crashed into the North Sea this afternoon with the loss of all 432 passengers and crew. No explanation for the crash has yet been suggested; it is hoped that when the black flight box has been recovered it may give some guidance to the investigation team, which is already on its way. . . .

"The body of the middle-aged woman who fell to her death on the London-to-Midchester railway line this afternoon has been identified as Miss Mitchell-Matthiesson, a magistrate and member of several governing bodies who also had a seat on the HNEA Board of Education. . . ."

* * *

Now I'll *never* get it back, was my first thought. And my second was, Well, at least I shan't have the job of explaining to Fred. Though, dammit, it was he who picked my pocket first.

But the trouble is, I really miss the old bastard. It seems dismally queer and lonely in the house without him.

Pearly has turned awkward and for some reason doesn't seem to want to see me.

Also, I keep thinking about that mother and kid. I can't see them anymore, but I know they are *there* all right. I can feel them, as I travel up and down to the airport stop, I can feel their empty hollow eye sockets turn and watch me as I chug past in the train. What are they waiting for?

Plainly it wasn't for old Meddlesome Matty.

And—do you know . . . I've discovered who the girl reminds me of. Why, it's Ma! Rummaging about in some old drawers the other day, for want of anything better to do, I came across a photo of Ma the way she must have been, long before Fred and I remember her —quite young, in her early twenties—and she was the spit image of that girl. Flowered droopy suit and all.

So, who was the kid in the push chair?

Our elder brother?

And what are they expecting *me* to do?

The Lame King

"Crumbling rainbows are useless as a diet," said Mrs. Logan. "I don't like 'em. Prefer something solid to bite on."

Under her breath, in the front passenger's seat, Mrs. Logan's daughter-in-law Sandra muttered, "Shut up, you dotty old bore." And, above her breath, she added to her husband, *"Can't* you drive a bit faster, Philip? It will be terribly late by the time we get home. There's the sitter's fee, don't forget. And we've got all our packing to do."

"You have all tomorrow to do it in," mildly pointed out her father-in-law from the backseat.

She flashed him an angry diagonal glance, and snapped, "There's plenty of other things to do, as well as packing. Cancel the milk, take Buster to the dog's hotel, fill out all the notification forms—"

"I would have done that, if you had let me," said old Mr. Logan in his precise tones. He had been a headmaster. Sandra made no answer at all to this, merely pressed her lips tight together and clenched her gloved hands in her lap. "Do drive faster, Philip," she said again.

44

Philip frowned and slightly shook his head, without taking his eyes off the road. He was tall and pale, with a bony righteous face and eyes like faded olives. "Can't; you know that perfectly well; it's illegal to go over sixty with senior citizens in the car," he said in a low voice.

His remark was drowned, anyway, by the voice of his mother, old Mrs. Logan, who called from the back, "Oh, no, don't drive faster, Philip dear, please don't drive any faster! I am so *loving* the landscape—I don't want to lose a moment of it! Our heroine, speeding to who knows where, or what destination, is reminded of childhood— those bare trees, the spring mornings passed paddling in brooks when the water went over the tops of your wellies—the empty fields—"

Old Mr. Logan gently took her hand in his, which had the effect of checking her.

"It *is* a pretty country," he said. "I like all the sheep. And the shapes of the hills around here."

"How much farther?" said Sandra to her husband.

"About another four hours' driving. We'd better stop for a snack at a Cook's Tower."

"Oh, why?" Sandra said crossly, in a low tone. "It's just a waste of money giving them a—"

"No wolves now. It must have been so exciting for shepherds in the old days," dreamily remarked old Mrs. Logan. "Virginia came down like a wolf on the . . . but then when you try and fold on the dotted line it *never* tears straight. That is one thing they should put right in the next world."

"And I'm sure they will," said her husband comfortingly.

"I hope my thoughts are not without sense."

45

"Never to me, my love. Look at that farm, tucked so snugly in the hollow."

"Will the place we are going to be like that?"

"Anyway the tank needs filling," said Philip to his wife.

"What this trip will have *cost,*" she muttered.

"It had to be taken sometime. And we'll get the termination grants, don't forget," Philip reminded his wife in a murmur.

"Well, but then you have to deduct all the expenses—"

"Sometimes I think my daughter-in-law treads in the footsteps of Sycorax," absently remarked old Mrs. Logan, who sometimes caught Sandra's tone, though not the things she actually said.

"Oh, come, you would hardly call little Kevin a Caliban?" mildly remonstrated her husband.

"Parting from little Kevin is the least of my regrets. He is all the chiefs and none of the Indians. And stubborn! Combs his hair five times and then says 'I don't want to go.'"

"Kevin will grow up by and by. If he were a character in one of your books, you would know how to make him grow up."

"Ah," she said with a sigh, "no story would grow in my hands now. It would fly apart in a cloud of feathers. You say a few words—and they come back and hit you like boomerangs. What did Western man do before he knew about the boomerang? What did swallows do before they invented telegraph wires? Language is so inexact—I do not mean to assert that swallows themselves invented the wires—"

"For God's *sake,* shut up," muttered young Mrs. Lo-

gan in the front seat. Old Mr. Logan laid an arm protec-
tively round his wife's shoulders. She, with an alert,
happy face, white hair flying about in wisps, continually
gazed out the window as the car sped along. "Haven't
seen so much grass in ten years," she whispered. Her
elderly husband looked at her calmly and fondly. Sometimes a shadow of pain flitted across his face, like that of
a high jet over a huge field, but it was gone the moment
after.

"There's a place," said Philip. "We'll stop there."

A Cook's Tower had come in sight: square white
pillar, castellated at the top, with red zigzags all the way
down, and a wide parking lot glittering with massed
vehicles.

"Park somewhere close in, we don't want to waste
twenty minutes helping them hobble," muttered
Sandra.

"I'll park as close as I can," replied Philip with a
frown, and called to the pair in the back, "Fancy a snack,
Mum and Dad? Cup o' tea? Sandwich?"

He tried to make his voice festive.

"Oh, there's no need for that, my boy," said his father. "We're all right, we're not hungry. Save your
money." But his mother called, "Oh, yes! A nice cup of
tea and a last rock cake. Rock of ages cleft for me. . . . A
book called *The Last Rock Cake*, now . . . that would
have been a certain seller, once; these days, I suppose,
The Last Croissant. Take the queen *en croissant;* a husband in Bohemia would be a Czech mate. Oh, cries his
poor silly wife, I am nothing but a blank Czeque; good
for nothing but to be wheeled away to the death house."

"*Will* you be quiet, Mother?" gritted Sandra, turning to the rear of the car a face of real ferocity.

4 7

"Never mind, my dear, you won't have us for much longer. It has been a stony row, I know, but tomorrow this time you will be en route for Ibiza—"

Philip, who had been weaving watchfully through the parking lot, eyes veering sharply this way and that, now whipped his Algonquin neatly into a just-vacated gap close to the main entrance.

Inside, at this time of day, the Quick Snak cafeteria was half empty; most customers were up on the top floor having the three course special.

"You sit here."

Philip edged his parents alongside a glass-topped table by the window.

"Sandra and I will forage at the counter. What's it to be? Buttered toast?"

"A rock cake," sighed Mrs. Logan. "Just a rock cake. To remind me of our honeymoon in Lynmouth."

Mr. Logan said he wanted nothing but a cup of tea. He placed a careful hand to his side. Mrs. Logan noticed this and sighed again, but said nothing.

Their table was littered with crumby plates, crumpled paper napkins, half-empty cups, and, on the windowsill, a grease-smeared, dog-eared paperback.

"Why, look, my dear," said old Mr. Logan, turning it over. "It's one of yours. *The Short Way Back*. Now, isn't that a remarkable coincidence. A good omen, wouldn't you say?"

They gazed at each other, delighted.

"I was only twenty-five when I wrote that one," sighed his wife. "Philip already on the way. . . . How could I *do* it? What came into my head? *Now*, I couldn't. . . ."

She handled the book gently, affectionately, smiling at the absurd picture on the front.

"Nothing at all to do with what's inside. But then, whatever is?"

A small old man, limping, passed by their table. His heavy metal tray held a glass of stout, black, froth-topped, and a shiny Bath bun.

"*That* looks good," said Mrs. Logan to him confidentially. "Now I'm sorry I didn't ask for stout. And a Bath bun. . . . Do you know what? We found, we actually found a book I once wrote, lying here on the windowsill. Now isn't that a thing!"

"Well, I never!" The man with the stout beamed at her. "So you're a book writer, are you?" His voice had a slight regional burr. Welsh? wondered Mr. Logan. Or Scottish?

"Was once. In those *jeunesse dorée* days. Do re me, lackaday dee—" she sang softly.

"He sipped no sup and he craved no crumb," joined in the old man with the tray, "as he sighed for the love of a lady."

"Why!" exclaimed Mrs. Logan in astonished pleasure. "Now you remind me—you remind me of somebody I once knew—"

"I was just thinking the very same thing!" said her husband. "But who—?"

All three looked at one another in excitement and suspense.

"Now, when was it, where was it?" murmured Mrs. Logan.

But at this moment Philip came back with a tray, followed by Sandra, with another.

"Excuse *me,*" he said with brisk chill, and the old man with the stout moved quickly on his way.

"*Really,* Mother," snapped Sandra, "must you get into conversation with all and sundry?" and she thumped down in front of her mother-in-law a thick china plate on which lay a flat pale macaroon, ninety-percent gray pastry, with a flat wan dob of fawn-colored substance in the middle.

"Oh, but I asked for a rock cake. This isn't—"

"No rock cakes. Only jam tarts, buns, or macaroons."

Mrs. Logan drank her tea but declined the macaroon. "Too hard on my teeth. *You* have it, love." So Philip ate it, after his ham roll, with a harassed air of doing so only because it had been paid for and must not go to waste. Sandra nibbled a salad which was largely cress. She looked repeatedly at her watch.

"Philip, we should be getting on. Need the ladies', Mother? You'd better, you don't know what there will be at—"

Rather reluctantly Mrs. Logan rose to her feet and followed her daughter-in-law to the pink boudoir, peppered over with hearts and cupids.

"Sandra," she said—for the first time a slight tremor entered her voice—"Sandra, will it be *frightening,* do you think—where we're going?"

Sandra angrily banged at her nose with a makeup puff and skated a comb through her perm. "Frightening? Why should it? Everyone's got to go through it sometime, haven't they? Not just you. We'll have to, too, Philip and me, when our turn comes. There's nothing *frightening* about it. Come along—the others will be waiting. Hurry up!"

Philip and his father waited at the window table.

Philip had impatiently piled together all the used cups, plates, napkins, and the paperback book, without observing its title.

"Women take so long, always," he muttered. "Can't think what they get up to."

The limping old man passed their table again and nodded in a friendly way at Mr. Logan.

"On the way to Last House, are you?"

"Why should you ask that?" said Philip sharply.

"Many who stop here are going that way. There's a bad greasy patch at the S-bend going over Endby Hill— you want to watch it there. Quite a few have come off at that corner."

"Thank you," said old Mr. Logan. "We'll remember."

Philip gave a curt nod, as if he needed no lame old strangers to teach him about careful driving, and Mr. Logan added cheerfully,

"It'd be a piece of irony, wouldn't it, if just when you were taking us—*there*— we all went off the road and ended up together!"

"Father! *Really!*"

"Little Kevin would have to go into an orphanage."

"Here come the girls," said Philip, with a jocularity he did not feel.

"What's that about an orphanage?" inquired his mother, who, her husband noticed, had a drawn and anxious look on her face. She plunged into the conversation as if trying to distract her own mind. "They say many a home is worse than an orphanage. Remember, some also agree that impatience is the worst sin. I suffered from it myself, to an extreme degree, when I was young. . . ."

"Come along, let's go," said Philip, showing signs of suffering from the worst sin himself.

A frail dusk had begun to fall as they resumed their journey. The landscape became ghostly, wreathed in layers of mist. Trees loomed, fringed by creepers, then swung past; the road wound uphill through forest.

"I wonder if there will be a view?" murmured old Mrs. Logan, more to herself than to her companions. Her husband took her hand, holding it close and firmly. She went on, still to herself, "He was always delighted with your comments on landscape, chaffinches, and so forth; I wonder if he would be still? That was a curious encounter, a curious coincidence. Candied apple, quince and plum and gourd. . . . I wonder what candied *gourd* would be like? Not very nice, I'd think. But then the whole of that picnic sounded decidedly sickly— lucent syrups tinct with cinnamon: *not* what one would wish on one's bed in the middle of the night."

"Please be quiet, Mother," said Philip edgily. "There's a bad place along here, we were warned about it; I don't want any distraction, if you would be so kind."

"Of course, Philip, of course. I am so very sorry, I know I am a nuisance to you."

The bad place was negotiated, and passed, in complete silence. The elderly pair at the back drew close together in the darkness until they seemed like one person. The headlights in front converged to a sharp white V through the foggy murk.

At last the car rolled to a stop.

"Is this the place?" Mrs. Logan's voice quavered a very little.

"This is it."

Philip, relieved at having completed the outward trip, stamped to get the stiffness out of his knees; his voice was rather too cheerful. "Come along, Mother, Dad; we'll just get you registered, then we must be on our way; we're going to have to hurry to get home by the time the sitter wants to leave—"

The old people crept awkwardly out from the back of the car.

"One thing, there's no luggage to bother about," muttered Sandra. "But you would think they'd make these places more accessible—"

The small group of persons passed inside a building which was so closely surrounded by creeper-hung trees of large size that, in the foggy dark, no architectural detail was visible; it was like walking into a grove, Mrs. Logan thought.

The elderly pair clung together, hand clasped tightly in hand, while forms were filled out at the desk.

Then—

"Well, we'll be leaving you now, then, Mum and Dad," said Philip, falsely hearty. "Cheerio! Take care! All the best. Bon voyage, and all that." He gave them each a peck on the cheek. Sandra muttered something inaudible, and the younger pair walked hastily out through the front entrance.

"Whooo!" Philip muttered, after a moment, slamming the car into gear. "Wouldn't want to go through *that* again in a hurry."

"Now," hissed his wife, "now will you *please* drive at a reasonable speed? No more dawdling, if you please. There's a whole *lot* to do when we get home."

"All right, all right—" and he accelerated so sharply that the engine let out a squawk of protest.

Old Mr. and Mrs. Logan were led in different directions.

"But can't we be together?" she protested.

"No. We are very sorry, but that is an absolute rule. There is nothing to worry about, though—"

They gave each other a cold, steady kiss, aged cheek against soft aged cheek.

"Now, then, where?"

Mrs. Logan was taken to a kind of garden room. One wall was totally lacking; darkness, trees, and mist lay beyond the area of dim illumination.

"If you wouldn't mind just waiting here. . . . He won't be long."

"Will it be Ted's turn first, or mine?"

No answer came back, Or had the guide perhaps said, "Both together?" as the door closed?

Mrs. Logan sat on a bench, looking out anxiously into the dark.

It isn't very cold, she thought. Not as cold as you'd expect. Not cold at all, really. Cold blows the wind tonight, true love. . . . Wasn't that queer, though, finding that book? Then tell to me, my own true love, when shall we meet again? When the autumn leaves that fall from the trees, Are green and spring again. Yes, but *do* they spring again? Leaves, like the things of man you with your fresh thoughts care for, can you? Always dwell as if about to depart, they say in Yorkshire. Do they depart so easily, up there, in Yorkshire? Questions are better than answers, for they lead you on, like signposts, whereas answers pin you down, like javelins. Will Ted remember to tell them about his diet?

Somebody was approaching through the darkness, walking slowly and carefully; the sound of the footfalls came with an irregular beat, as if the person limped.

Vulcan, thought Mrs. Logan; Richard III. Beware the lame king, for then shall Sparta fall. But the lame god is kind, he knows our frailties all . . . that line does not scan as it should. One foot too many, like a three-legged stool. Or too few . . .

"There you are, then," said the old lame man. "I brought you a glass of stout and a Bath bun."

"So it was you, all along?"

She gazed at him in amazement.

"All along."

"All along," she echoed happily, "down along, out along lee."

"That's it!"

And they began to sing together, their voices combining gently in old, remembered graceful cadences. Oh, I hope Ted is as happy as this! she thought.

Far away, from Endby Hill, the sound of a long-drawn-out crash came faintly through the foggy dark. But neither of the singers paid it any heed.

The Jealous Apprentice

Of course the academy of which my aunt Gwen is dean can't be spoken of by its true name. Graduates refer to it affectionately as Crib College. But its full title is the Antient & Singular Academie of Farcing, Charmerie, Prigging Law, and Cracksmanship. There are no written records kept, naturally, but the college has been in existence, one way or another, since the fifteenth century, and very probably much longer. It moves about the country, since a permanent headquarters would be undesirable; under Henry VIII was the longest tenure of one spot, an expropriated monastery, but then some up-and-coming nobleman moved in, and the staff and students moved out, hastily, by night.

Courses, naturally, have changed during the centuries; dummering, swadding, and demanding for glimmer are no longer on the syllabus; but the black art (lock picking), lifting law (parcel stealing) and motor-prad law (theft of wheeled vehicles) are still on the regular timetable and form part of the basic groundwork of lore which students are expected to absorb in their first year. They are not, in fact, referred to as students; early us-ages still obtain in the college and novices for their first seven years are bound by strict agreements of indenture, and are known as apprentices. Then they serve a further two years as journeymen.

After this period they are formally invested with the black velvet mask, fine steel chain, and gilt nutcrackers of the master cracksman. However, as the conditions of service are somewhat hazardous, it is doubtful whether more than about thirty percent of apprentices ever work through to full mastership. Those that do so are principally in the more studious and sedentary branches, cursitor work, forging, Barnard's law, cheating at cards, and, nowadays, computer scripping and tax versing. But, since apprentices are sent out to cribs with the more experienced journeymen (as, of course, they must be, or how will they ever acquire experience?) if the peelers should rumble the ken and arrive on the spot, it is college law that the santer, or apprentice, shall if possible help his journeyman to escape (with the pelfry if he can) and allow himself to be taken, in order to let his senior get clear. Apprentices are not so nimble at getting away and at most periods, therefore, the ranks of the second-, third-, and fourth-year students are thinned because many of them will be in the clink, or pokey. (Their fees are remitted during this time.)

It is, of course, unusual for a woman to be dean of the college and indeed my aunt Gwen Thornbush was the first female to be so honored as far as the verbal annals record. But the college was founded by a famous wild rogue, Wat Thornbush, about whom there are no proved tales but innumerable legends, and there has always been a member of the Thornbush tribe to continue the tradition ever since. Lambert Thornbush, Gwen's great-grandfather, was one of the last highwaymen, or high-lawyers, who achieved a highly correct and exemplary end, being hanged at Tyburn; her grandfather was caught prigging a gross of gold snuffboxes from the Pavilion at Brighton, and was transported to Botany Bay; her great-uncle, branching into more intellectual pursuits, made a very comfortable fortune by fraudulent company promotion.

The college does not advertise. And its current whereabouts, at any one time, are not widely known. Would-be students must be endowed with pertinacity and firm intentions, they must pass through a lengthy channel of inquiry and referral, question and answer, all by word of mouth, before they, so to speak, even reach the porter's lodge. There has been only one instance of a peeler's spy, or smoke, managing to bluff his way in and enter as a student. What happened to him has passed into legend and is a deterrent for any member of the academy who might consider blabbing on a fellow practitioner or grassing to the police about college activities: it began with having his tongue burned out by hot irons and went on for five days. Apprentices, when they sign their indentures, take what is known as the *Bitter Oath*, which binds them for life as the Hippocratic Oath does members of the medical profession.

There are, of course, as well as the regular syllabus, weekend courses, seminars, refresher courses, and high-pressure intensive classes to keep graduates up to the minute in new techniques such as laser work and computer fraud. My aunt Gwen was herself a computer expert—she had done that beautiful little job on meat supplies for Whiplash Worldwide hamburger bars which netted her a cool million; she could easily have retired, and indeed she invested much of the money in new equipment for the college; but my aunt was a natural hard worker and enjoyed practicing the art for its own sake; she often voiced her ambition to die in harness like Great-Grandfather Lambert. She did not, however, very often go out on a crib herself. The case I am going to relate was one of the rare exceptions.

It was an unusual mark altogether. In the first place, my aunt was approached by an outsider, a simpler, which is extremely uncommon. After a series of messages a meeting was arranged at a small Indian restaurant in a medium-sized northern town of no interest called Bucklawrie. Confidence was rapidly established between my aunt, a shrewd judge of character, and the simpler, who identified himself as a member of a distinguished north-country family. His errand was an odd one. It seemed that the family mansion was to be sold up. This was partly a matter of necessity. He explained that the house, Normanby Priory, was disastrously situated on a ridge, underneath which a whole series of coal shafts had been dug (in fact it was from these mines that the Normanby family had made their very substantial fortunes). Somewhat shortsightedly, they had not, in burrowing for riches underground, realized the hazard to the family home, custom built for them on the ruins of the ancient abbey by the Adam brothers and custom furnished by Sheraton; but now the mines had been nationalized, the family had fallen on hard times, and the National Trust refused to take on the mansion, which was about to fall in half, if not vanish entirely into a huge crack which was opening across the hillside. The coal shafts, now worked out, could not be filled in because of the danger from springs of water; the only course was to abandon the house and realize the value of its contents. This value, of course, was immense: furnished at the heyday of the family's prosperity, the priory contained treasures of every possible kind, paintings by Raeburn, Romney, Rembrandt, and Goya, tapestries, china, gold, marble, jewelry and antiques of all periods. What my aunt's customer wanted was nothing much; he introduced himself as Cyril Normanby, a younger brother in a cadet branch of the family. He would not, he said, be personally benefiting in any way by the sale of the contents, and he was angry about it: Lord Normanby, his cousin, was selling all the family treasures to overseas collectors and nothing would be left in this country. He felt it a slur on the family honor and was resolved that one article, at least, should be saved from this wholesale dispersal. What did he intend to do with it? Well, he said, in his lifetime it would remain hidden in his London flat, a source of comfort and solace to him (he was not a young man); after his death it would go to the National Gallery, he would make provision in his will. My aunt did not discuss the legality of this; that was not her province; she had, apparently, taken a fancy, as strong-minded women sometimes will, to the frail elderly man opposite her picking distastefully at his gingery curry. She accepted the commission, named her fee, a thumping one, which he paid on the spot, with a credit card, and the deal was agreed.

"When do you want it done?" she inquired.

The house, he told her, was in process of being cleared. Silver and china had gone already. A firm of art transporters would be calling in three weeks to remove the paintings; so there was no time to lose. The article that Mr. Normanby wished to reserve for himself was a small painting by Goya; a portrait of an ancestress, Lady Maria Normanby, whose father had been British ambassador at the Escorial. "It is a very beautiful painting," he said wistfully. "And moreover it is exactly like my dear mother who died twenty years ago."

My aunt Gwen noted the particulars of the painting, and whereabouts in the house it was hung, and the client gave her a great deal more information about the priory, in which he had grown up. Then the pair parted.

Aunt Gwen was somewhat exercised in her mind as to whether to undertake the crib herself or allow one of her journeymen-students to do so. Normally, since it was a rather superior piece of lifting, she would have done it; but lately she had been suffering from acute arthritis in the neck and shoulders (arthritis is an unfortunate occupational hazard of foisting, nipping, and all outdoor forms of knavery due to the long hours spent motionless, watching, in damp exposed spots); naturally my aunt would not let herself be deterred by such a small consideration as a little pain, but she was afraid that the affliction might impair her efficiency.

She therefore, after much thought, entrusted the job to her senior journeyman student, an extremely proficient troll and prigger, Tom Casewit, who had only six months remaining before he would have completed the full course and be a master cracksman. Tom was a silent, taciturn individual, dark, with a scarred cheek, result of a turnup with the slops; his final graduation had been delayed by a four-year sentence in the pokey but he had not wasted his time while in jail as he had the good luck there to encounter a famous Australian safe-breaker who taught him some elegant variations of method.

"It's not a hard job, Tom," Aunt Gwen told him.

"There's no one living in the house at night now. You can do it on your own—you won't need a warp or a stand."

Warps and stands keep watch outside. And the gin who opens the window is called a tricker.

"You need not take your apprentice," Gwen told Tom. "The house is only protected by electric alarms; and any first-year can deal with *them.*"

Tom nodded. He was never one for unnecessary words.

"It seems a bit odd that they should leave the big house empty," Miss Thornbush went on, "even though it's liable to fall into the coal mine down below within the next six months, you'd think there'd be plenty of markers and curbers keen to get in and hook up the pickings. But apparently that's not so. The reason why is—"

At this point she dropped her voice, which was not loud at the best of times. A hidden listener, who was curled up under a loose floorboard in Miss Thornbush's study, strained his ears, but to his great annoyance was unable to hear what she said next. Some word like *glaar*? The *glaar* keeps them away? That was what it sounded like; but there is no such word in the language.

A moment later the door opened and closed; Tom Casewit had gone out. And not long after Miss Thornbush followed him; and presently the listener uncurled himself and pushed up the floorboard and made his escape.

Who was this listener? Why, it was Tom's apprentice, Skin Masham; a thin, hollow-eyed boy, so bony and gangling in appearance that his skill in creeping through narrow places was continually amazing his fellow students; he could slip through a crack that seemed hardly wide enough to pass a chisel or a picklock through. Where a ray of moonshine could go, Skin Masham could follow, they used to say. He had a tuneful voice, too, and could sing the college song very movingly:

> Oh, when I am dead and go to my grave
> A flashy funeral let me have
> Let none but bold robbers carry my corpse
> And sing, "There goes a wild 'un, a wild
>   and wicked warp!"

But despite his voice and his agility, Skin Masham was not popular with the students; he had a spiteful, jealous nature, was always fancying himself overpassed and put upon; he felt that nobody gave him his due, and he hated, he hated with the whole strength of his nature, anybody who had something that he wanted. An apprentice was supposed to serve his journeyman faithfully, stand below the window with the wresters, hold the curb, carry the garbage to the marker, watch at all times for the peelers, and, if necessary, interpose himself and hold them up while the senior prigger made his escape. So far, such a crisis had not arisen; but it seemed highly unlikely that Skin would act in so self-sacrificing a manner should it be required. Tom Casewit did not wholly trust him; but then, Tom Casewit trusted nobody.

Gnawing his nails to the quick, Skin crept away down the passage. He was consumed with jealousy that Tom should be sent away to a crib without him. Normanby Priory was quite evidently a first-class crib, a really grand one; it would have counted at least thirty credits to him in his end-of-term marking. Why should

Tom have all the credit—Tom who would be a journey-man soon in any case? It was unfair—hideously unfair!

Skin decided to take action on his own. He would show the old bag who in her ropey old college was a really skillful cracksman. And if he could put a spoke in Tom's wheel at the same time, why, so much the better.

Students of the college were, of course, expected to study a crib intensively before attempting to crack it. Movements of inmates, arrivals of outside tradesmen, resident animals and their habits, surrounding vegeta-tion, local weather conditions, even folklore if relevant —all had to be absorbed and taken into account.

Tom Casewit had immediately gone off on what was known as tolling time; Skin went to Miss Thornbush and asked for leave of absence to attend the wedding of a sister in New Haven, Connecticut.

"You must be exceedingly fond of your sister to want to go such a distance?" remarked Miss Thornbush look-ing at him skeptically over the tops of her steel glasses. Skin did not seem the kind for deep family attachments.

"Oh, it's just, ma'am—we haven't seen each other since we was kinchins." Skin tried to look properly wist-ful; actually he loathed his sister, who was married to a wealthy bookmaker, and would not have gone within fifty miles of her house.

"Very well; you may have two weeks. But you had better study your theory of termage and quitteries while you are away—if you expect to pass the Lent term exam-inations," his principal told him sternly.

Skin escaped, muttering spitefully, packed a small bag, and hitched a ride to Kinnockshire, in which county, he had discovered by study in the college li-brary, Normanby Priory was to be found.

The Jealous Apprentice

Kinnockshire is a wild, rugged county. The inhabitants speak a dialect hardly changed from the ninth century, when the valleys were overrun by Norsemen who stayed for a while, decided that the climate was too bleak to be endured, and returned home again. Toward the north angle of the county, which is one of the smallest in England, Kinnockdale lies between two gloomy crags; and, at the foot of Kinnockdale, Normanby Priory is uncomfortably perched on top of its coal mines.

Watching the house was not easy. In such a countryside, a stranger sticks out like a cactus in a cabbage bed; Skin had to steal a bicycle, and make do with cycling through daily, in different disguises: sometimes a punk, sometimes a boy scout, sometimes a messenger on special delivery. He found that, as Miss Thornbush had said, the house stood empty, except for the staff engaged on the daily work of dismantling and removal. It was a big gray place, on its green slope of hill; very plain, Skin thought it.

He tried asking local people about it, but their accent wholly defeated him; and as for the *glaar*, if that indeed was the word that Miss Thornbush had used, at the end of ten days he had reached no further conclusion about what it could be. Probably some kind of weather: mist or fog or wind coming across the fells. It was a cold, gloomy countryside. One story Skin finally did manage to translate out of the local dialect, which only confirmed his feelings about the place: back there some time in history, two, three hundred years ago, the couple who lived in the place at the time, Lord and Lady Normanby of that date, had starved their daughter to death, one of their daughters; just took and shut her up in a room and starved her, because she refused to marry somebody they thought she ought; either that, or she wanted to marry some unsuitable young fellow of her own. So they let her die of hunger in her own bedroom. What do you think of that! Skin reckoned that such folk deserved to have their house fall into a coal mine and lose all their money; anything that he could prig from the house before the contents were all dispersed seemed like fair pickings.

Quite soon he spotted what must be Tom Casewit; it was a good disguise, he must acknowledge, an old dame rigged up as an archaeologist from Newcastle University with field glasses and all kinds of measuring implements, limping about in the grounds of the priory peering at barrows and piles of stones. The ground was all cracked and heaved up, like molehills on a big scale; you could believe that, quite soon, the whole house would go crashing down into the black caves underneath. Jeez; what a spooky notion. Skin decided that he had reconnoitered quite long enough; he'd go in tonight, bag the painting of Lady Maria and any other little items he chanced across, then get the obloquium out of there.

At dusk he called the local slops. Putting on his sister's voice, which he could mimic very cleverly, he told them that the lady archaeologist was really a high-class cracksman, and that if they looked in her knapsack they'd find wall-climbing kit and a magnetic neutralizer for dowsing electronic burglar alarms. "Who is this?" the police-station operator naturally said, but Skin rang off at that point; however, they had paid serious attention to what he told them and, later, hiding in a gully in the priory grounds, he was delighted to observe them arrive and do a snatch on the old archaeologist dame. And— what a surprise!—when they took off her wig, it wasn't

Tom Casewit at all, but old Miss Gwen, Miss Thornbush the principal; she must have decided to do the prig herself after all. Skin did feel a trifle nervous at that; shopping Tom was one thing, that would have troubled him not a whit; but to do in the Old Lady Troll herself, that was a bit shattering and more than he had bargained for. How would he deal with the simpler on his own? And who would take on the deanship and give him his degree in due course? Still, no use crossing bridges before he came to them. The first thing was to do this prig.

Skin entered the priory as easily and as skillfully as a field mouse, nipping through the crack of a rotting door; he had of course put his quietus on the burglar alarm first, and the slops were no doubt by this time off at the slop-ken interrogating old Troll Thornbush, and long might they keep her there!

Slipping up the carpetless stairway, silent as a cloud of dust, Skin made his way to the picture gallery.

Along at the east end, the old simpler had told Miss Thornbush and she had told Tom Casewit: a picture of a lady in a gray dress and a pearl necklace.

Easy to spot. Couldn't mistake it.

The night was cloudy, not dark, and by the time he reached the end of the gallery his eyes were accustomed. He could see the outline of the picture well enough, and make out that it was a bird, with hair done on top of her head and a strand or two of cobbles round her neck; jeez, what a size! Pity they weren't real ones, they'd be a sight better worth prigging than an old bit of painted canvas.

About to lift down the canvas, Skin had a bad fright; a voice behind him whispered, "Here you are at last!"

He spun round, pretty fast, at that, you may be sure; and was not pleased to see a dame standing as close to him as he was to the picture.

"Who by the troll are you?" says he, staring at this nan, as well he might; for in nearly all respects she was the image of the picture: dressed all in gray, with her hair done up on top and the rope of cobbles round her neck. The only difference was in her face, which looked like all of hunger itself; the eyes, the gaping mouth, the fallen-in cheeks, the ravenous despairing gaze she fixed on him, were all enough to set the cold prickles coursing down his back.

"Who am I?" says she. "Don't you know me, and I've waited for you here for so long? I am the glaar," she says, and with that she steps forward and takes him by the hands, both hands, for he was so bedazed he couldn't fend her off; he lets out a little pitiful whimper, like a puppy as you wring its neck; and then a crack opens in the floor and down they go, both of them, and the walls as well, pictures, carpets, and the lot, with a rumble and tumble of falling masonry. And that was the end of Skin Masham, and the end of Normanby Priory as well; by the time the art transporters arrived there was nothing to be seen but a big hole in the ground, and if anyone has gone down into the mine to hunt for all those pictures and Sheraton chairs, they haven't found them yet.

If you ask me, Skin Masham was lucky; what he'd have got from his fellow students for shopping the principal would have lasted far longer and been a whole lot more painful than falling down a crack with a ghost.

What happened to Miss Gwen Thornbush? Serving a short sentence for being apprehended with burglars' tools.

The Jealous Apprentice

Who's running the academy? Why, I am.

Toby Thornbush, transported to Botany Bay, was my great-uncle. Bug-Eye Casewit, my grandfather, was a famous bushranger, Toby's brother-in-law; so when sentence was passed, Aunt Gwen said to me: "Tom, you'll keep an eye on the kids till I'm out, won't you?"

Always one to keep things running and do her duty, Aunt Gwen; that was why she'd decided she had better face the glaar, and not send a deputy to do it. Anyway, I reckon, as things turned out it was all for the best; that Skin Masham was no loss.

A Rhyme
for Silver

Eighteen-year-old Jeff Tichborne worked in Goodman's TV and radio repair department. His younger brother Simon always enjoyed passing the shop window, which was brilliantly lit and packed with television screens, curved colored glass rectangles, each showing a different picture of distant places all over the globe and what was going on there—football matches, volcanoes erupting, yachts capsizing, people planting rice, waterfalls, great bulldozers chewing away at the desert.

"It's like a live atlas," Simon said contentedly, leaning back in the wheelchair as Aunt Jean pushed him homeward. She took Simon to the clinic three days a week: what was done for him there didn't seem to help, in fact it made him feel worse, but they said it was for his benefit so he supposed he must put up with it good temperedly. In the end it would make little difference, but perhaps by then they would have learned facts that would help other people.

Simon lay back, consciously relaxing to quell the choked feeling that arose from treatment at the clinic, and looking forward to the evening. Evenings never varied: Jeff read aloud—poetry, his own or other people's—and if there was a travel film on TV they looked at it.

Simon was small and dark-haired and very calm; he liked to laugh, too, and found a lot of things surprisingly funny, but few people knew that, apart from Jeff and Aunt Jean. Simon worried sometimes about Jeff, but kept the worry to himself: only the future could untie *that* knot.

Jeff came home at six in a bad temper.

"Old Goodman says I take too long on repair jobs, doing them too carefully," he growled, shoveling down hamburger and fries. *"He* says it doesn't pay off—all I need to do is just join two ends together."

Simon watched his skinny, active, red-haired brother nostalgically. Once he, too, could have eaten hamburger and fries, but not anymore; thin soup or milk was his lot now, day in day out.

"You mustn't go against Mr. Goodman, Jeffie," said Aunt Jean, all of a twitter. She was a pale wispy woman with hair in a shiny net. "Not the way things are, with—with the rent rise and prices going up all the time. You have to do the job his way."

"I know, I know," said Jeff, slamming tea into his mug. Jeff's earnings had supported the family since Mr. and Mrs. Tichborne had been killed in a bus crash on the M 5 two years ago. His college plans had to be put off, perhaps permanently, for Aunt Jean's time was mainly spent on looking after Simon, and would be even more, quite soon.

"Goodman's full of slime—he's like an overripe puffball. One minute smarming the customers, next minute telling me to skimp on the job. And then he'll ask after

Sim in that oozy sugary voice. 'How's the little fellow getting on? Is he any better?' Ugh! he makes me sick!"

"What's your parrot's name?" said Sim softly, and Jeff burst into an unwilling guffaw, remembering the time last summer when Mr. Goodman had come with the truck to pick him up for an emergency repair. There had been an owl on the draining board: Jeff had found it, stunned, in Dyeworks Lane the previous evening, and Sim, who loved wild creatures and was clever with them, had dressed a wound on its wing and given it brandy. Two days later it was well enough to fly away, but in the meantime Mr. Goodman, calling, had mistaken it for a parrot.

"He asked after the parrot, just last week. I said it had flown away."

"What did he say?"

"Oh, what a shame. The little fellow ought to have a pet."

"A nice fluffy kitten with a blue ribbon," suggested Sim.

Then they watched a film about the Amazon, and, after it finished, Jeff read aloud his latest which was called "Group Therapy," and Sim made some useful criticisms. Then, as he often did, Sim asked for Chidiock Tichborne's poem, and Jeff read that.

Next Sunday afternoon Sim was out in the front garden in his wheelchair, making a careful drawing of Mrs. Trevor's Labrador, Sootie, who lay heaving in the sun on the next-door lawn, when Mr. Goodman drove up in the truck to collect Jeff for another urgent repair job.

"That's right, that's right," he said, giving Sim's drawing an indulgent glance. "Pretty good, eh?" Sim drew formidably well. "I suppose you'd like a doggie of your own, wouldn't you? What's your favorite sort?"

"No—I don't want a dog." Foreseeing all kinds of tiresomeness if Mr. Goodman took this notion into his head, Sim added quickly and absently, "I'd rather take a trip to Niagara." On the grass beside him lay a library book which contained six different painters' views of the waterfall; Sim had been thinking how very nice it would be to paint his own version, and add a seventh to the total. *That* would be a thing to leave behind. Sim knew that he was due to die, not very far in the future; he had grown accustomed to the prospect and didn't particularly mind it, but there were things he wanted to do first.

"A trip to Niagara? Well, I never!" said Mr. Goodman, quite taken aback. For the moment he was silenced. Later in the week, though, he told Jeff, "You ought to get your younger brother to Niagara if that's what he wants. After all, there isn't much—" He thought for a moment and added, "Maybe the local paper would do an appeal."

Jeff scowled without answering. He loathed the idea of charity.

"Do you really want to see Niagara so badly?" he asked Simon that evening.

"No, no; old Goodman got carried away by sentiment as usual." Just the same, he had a distant look in his eye that troubled his brother.

Jeff had read stories in the paper about dying children who longed to go to a Butlins camp or Buckingham Palace or Southend, and kind neighbors who clubbed together to arrange the treat. He found the idea a bit sickening. Fine for the neighbors who, no doubt, felt all puffed up with virtue and kindness. But what about the children, after the treat was over, when all they had was death to wait for? Had they really been done such a good turn?

Sim was different, of course: Sim was special. He had done such a lot of thinking in his life that in some ways he seemed the older of the two brothers.

Niagara, though! That was going to cost a fortune!

Jeff began thinking about ways of earning money. Then he saw the advertisement in the local paper: GUARD WANTED.

His annual three-week vacation was due. He had intended to spend it moonlighting, free-lancing on electrical repair jobs, but that would annoy Mr. Goodman very much if he got to hear of it, as he undoubtedly would; and the newspaper offer was not bad pay, eighty pounds a week. Two hundred and forty pounds with what Jeff had saved up . . .

He went and inquired about the job at the office of the local Nature Conservancy Board.

"You realize it would be a nonstop watching responsibility?" said Miss Plowright, the secretary of the board, who interviewed him. "We have guards alternating in twelve-hour shifts. And you have to stay right there, all the time. Five minutes away from the spot, and somebody could whip in; then all of the work would have been for nothing."

"Yes, I do see that," said Jeff, quite trembling with anxiety.

"What's your job—when you aren't doing guard work?" asked Miss Plowright, studying Jeff with curiosity. She thought he looked too thin and too angry, and

74

perhaps too imbued with imagination for his own good
—imagination that was never, or hardly ever, allowed
out for an airing.

She thought of moles, burrowing in the dark, with
their powerful claws: what happens to moles' claws if
they are not allowed to burrow?

"I—oh, I'm a poet," said Jeff absently. "I mean I'm an
electrician," he added next minute, blushing with fury.
He had been thinking how much he was going to enjoy
sitting out all night on the grassy hillside, thinking how,
for once, he would have *time* to think.

"A poet? Or an electrician?" Miss Plowright smiled
slowly. "Nothing to stop you being both."

"Well, I had an ancestor who was a poet. At least, he
wrote one poem."

Now, why had he told the woman that? But she did
not seem at all surprised; perhaps people often told her
things.

"Tichborne, Tichborne," she murmured. "I know
that name. Didn't he plot against the queen? And write
a very sad poem on the eve of his execution?"

"He was a Catholic, you see. He was only twenty-
eight when they executed him.

"My tale was heard, and yet it was not told
My fruit is fallen, yet my leaves are green—

"That's the one."

"He is certainly an ancestor to put you on your met-
tle," said Miss Plowright. "I can see it will be a job to live
up to him."

Jeff thought, recklessly, of telling her that they had
yet another ancestor, Elspeth Tichborne, accused of

witchcraft and burned at the stake, leaving, with her dying breath, such a curse on the judges who condemned her that all three died of the plague the following year. But he did not, and later was glad that he had not.

Miss Plowright was going on thoughtfully, "I can quite see why this kind of job had an appeal for you. What kind of poet are you?" And, as he looked blank, "Traditional or otherwise?"

"Oh, traditional."

"Regular meter? Rhyme?"

"Yes."

"Hmm, that's a pity."

"Why?"

"You might be so occupied trying to think of a rhyme that you would let the thieves get past you."

"I would not!" said Jeff, stung. Later he was to remember that too.

"All right, all right, I trust you!" she said. "And the job's yours. Night shift. I must say I do prefer rhyming poetry myself. Now, I'll tell you where to find the site. Here's a large-scale map. And don't, please, *don't* breathe a word to a single soul, not your nearest and dearest, *nobody*. This job is no joke, you know, it's deadly serious. We aren't paying out a hundred and sixty pounds a week just for fun."

"Not a single soul," promised Jeff, wondering how he was going to explain his nighttime activities to Sim and Aunt Jean.

But Miss Plowright said, "Of course, you can tell them that you are guarding a plant. But not just what and where. Or—seriously—you might be followed."

"It's like a spy story."

"It's almost worse. The things that selfish, greedy, uncaring people will do for money: or for rare specimens. In spite of the fact that there would be a fine of a thousand pounds for each plant stolen—very likely a prison sentence too. It's an endangered species, you see; there are only two known sites where it grows in England. Sad, really: when your ancestor wrote his poem there might have been hundreds of them, scattered all over the Downs. But, with plowing, and herbicides, and ignorant people who pick them—"

"And greedy, *un*-ignorant people who dig them up—"

"Yes, and of course they are also subject to the ordinary risks that affect any plant—they may be trodden on by cows, or nibbled by rabbits or flattened by motorbike scramblers. . . . Well, there you have it. Enjoy your watching. Recite your ancestor's poem, if you can't think up one of your own, and *keep awake.*"

Mr. Goodman dropped in one evening during Jeff's three-week leave.

"I know the lad's on vacation, but I thought as I knew he wasn't going away . . . and I reckoned he'd be pleased to pick up a bit of extra cash—"

It was another urgent repair job.

"I'm afraid my nephew's not here," said Aunt Jean, flustered.

"Ah? Out enjoying himself, is he? Don't blame him."

Sim thought dispassionately that Mr. Goodman's round pink face, with the little deep-sunk eyes like sparks, was like a fruit that has begun to decay, a soggy tomato with the stem sinking into a tiny wrinkled pit, and the flesh under the skin turning soft and rotten. For some obscure reason the look of it recalled Great-great-great-Grandmother Elspeth's curse: "I curse the lips that spake the sentence and the hard hearts that ordained it; I curse the hands that writ the accusation and the bodies that bore them; may they rot before the grave, and die before death take them, and roast in hellfire eternally thereafter. . . ."

"No—no, he's out on a job," twittered Aunt Jean. "To earn enough to send Simmie here away on a trip—"

Sim heaved a resigned sigh.

Mr. Goodman said, "Niagara! Yes, yes, of course! And a grand sight it'll be, young man, when you get there, it will indeed. Repair job?" probed Mr. Goodman sharply and delicately. "Not going behind my back to any of my customers, I hope?"

"No, no, of course not, not a repair job. Watching over a plant—"

Sim looked gravely at Aunt Jean, who bit her lip and shut up. But Mr. Goodman went right on probing.

"A plant, eh? That's interesting! One of those rare ones the World Wildlife folk are so hot on preserving? Funny, isn't it, really, they should spend so much on that when there's so much money wanted for other things—research on illness—like the lad here, and people dying of starvation in Africa and all the homeless. . . . Mind you, I'm keen on plants meself, got a nice few lilies and tropical orchids in my little greenhouse, they've no better specimens at Kew though I do say so—but you've got to have a sense of proportion, haven't you? Would it be an orchid, then, the boy's minding?"

"I can't say," said Aunt Jean faintly. "He never told us."

"Very right, very right. Very right. Can't trust anybody, these days. Maybe it'd be one of those monkey orchids, it's said they grow round here, up on Tillingham Down. *Very* uncommon, those are—there's a few more over in Berkshire, and that's all they know of. You'd like to see them, I daresay, wouldn't you, young man? You could make one of your drawings of them, maybe?"

"I'm not very good at drawing plants," Sim said politely.

"No? Well, I mustn't stand here with the grass growing under my feet! . . ."

Mr. Goodman trotted out, his pink face shining, paused for a word with Mrs. Trevor in her garden next door, who nodded and pointed to the right; then he shot off in his repair truck with the electric flashes in gold and green and GOODMAN'S LIGHTNING SERVICE blazoned along the side.

The first week passed quickly, and the second. There was, of course, an easy way up on to Tillingham Down: first the road until you came to Gamekeeper's Cottages, then across a farmyard past three silos, along by a wheatfield and up a chalk track beside a beechwood. But in order to foil possible observers, Jeff and his co-watcher, a dour chemistry student called Pat Jones from Leeds, adopted various roundabout routes to the site, scrambling up the side of the hill through the steep hanging woods, or right round to the back and across the racecourse, or up the Roman road two miles away eastward and so along the top of the ridge. Jeff began to know the little patch of woodland and the clearing where the orchid grew as well as his own front garden.

And the flowers? They were strange little twisted knots at the top of pale three-inch stems, tiny things, too unimportant looking to be deemed worthy of so much care and surveillance. They were withered, the flowering time was past—that was in May of course—and seed pods were already forming; but Miss Plowright had shown Jeff pictures, and then he had looked them up himself at home in the *Concise British Flora*. They were a purplish, reddish color, had two tiny legs, two tiny arms, a tail, a head with an infinitesimal darkish face— malevolent—two dots of green eyes and a kind of bishop's miter, three-pointed, in a lighter pink matching the pale pink stomach. A monkey bishop! Strangely enough, the little monkey-faces in the picture had a definite look of young Sim—there was something of his perky, detached quality in the way they stood springily on their stalks.

Jeff had grown to be very fond of them; he had a fatherly, protective attitude toward the withered little entities, waiting so mildly for their seed time and the end of summer. Here they had grown, here they waited, in this same hollow of downland, perhaps for hundreds of years, while kings came to the throne and went, while wars were fought, while Chidiock Tichborne wrote his poem and waited for the executioner, while Great-great-great-Grandmother reviled the bishops and judges, swore that she was innocent of the charges they laid against her, and then went up in flames.

Why are people so horrible to each other? Jeff wondered, sitting in the quiet dewy woods which were never completely silent at night, and never quite dark.

The sky, crammed with stars, hung low over the trees; then, long before sunrise, the stars faded and the sky brightened. Always, somewhere, there was something in motion—a twig snapping or a fan of leaves rustling. At first Jeff was nervous of these noises, expected wolves or bandits or boa constrictors, he hardly knew what. But soon he became accustomed to the sounds: they were just the night creatures of the woods, going about their business.

But why *are* people so horrible? They were no worse, those people in bygone days, than we are now. We are no more civilized than they were, we shoot and fight each other on the least excuse, we grab and steal what is not ours. Take the people who are after this little orchid. Why can't they leave it to grow in peace? How can somebody who has enough specialized knowledge to be aware of its value still be so callously selfish? You'd think that orchid hunters would be a cut above other collectors, but no, they are just as greedy and ruthless, just as ready to break laws and do irreparable damage.

"A plaguing mischief light on ye, hateful brigands!" Elspeth Tichborne had shouted, as they tied her to the stake. "My curse on the lot of ye! May the sun never warm ye, nor water quench your thirst. May the seeds shrivel that ye plant, and the food turn to gall in your bellies. I am innocent, and shall declare it to the last."

But they had burned her just the same.

In the third week, Sim caught a cold. This was serious for Sim had no resistance at all to germs, any bacillus that floated by could knock him endways. From germs at the clinic, of course, it was impossible to protect him, and Jeff privately thought that the clinic was the source of many of their problems; but this time it was indubitably Mr. Goodman, who dropped in one tea-time to inquire if Jeff would be free to come and rewire a church hall that evening.

"What? Still going off on those late-night outings? *We* know what to think when a young feller is out all night for weeks on end, don't we, Miss Tichborne?" With a wink. "Oh, I know, I know, he says he's watching over the monkey orchid—but we know better than that, don't we?"

"I never said anything about what I was doing," corrected Jeff.

"Nor you did! Nor you did. Just me going on. Why, if you were doing that, you'd not have to worry about raising cash to send the laddie to Niagara. They say there's collectors who'd pay thousands for a single seed pod."

Mr. Goodman fixed Jeff with an eye like a laser beam.

"Of *course* an honest young feller-me-lad like you, that does his work so carefully, would never pay any heed to types like that. HECK-tishooooo!" He gave a tremendous sneeze. "Got a bit of a cold, been out late too many nights meself—doing your work for you, young Jeff."

Squawking remonstrance, Aunt Jean almost pushed Mr. Goodman out of the kitchen. But the mischief was done: next day Sim was reduced to a limp flop of gasping misery, needed nonstop nursing and an oxygen cylinder in his room.

It was after three days of this, helping Aunt Jean nurse by day, watching by night, that Jeff one night fell asleep under his hawthorn spinney, while trying to think of a rhyme for silver. When he awoke, in the dripping hush of a gray and sodden dawn, the seed heads were gone. The monkey orchid stems had been clipped, very neatly, with scissors, close to the base.

For about ten minutes Jeff was numb with shock. He sat staring at the patch of ground: he literally found it impossible to believe his eyes. But there were the thirteen raw little stumps, and a couple of dark, bruised footprints in the rain-soaked turf. He found a crushed hollow in a nearby bramble-clump, where somebody had stood and waited. Jeff detested the thought of that, almost more than all else: that a person, his enemy, had stood there, watching, studying him, perhaps for several nights, waiting to pounce on the single moment of oblivion. And at last it had come. And Jeff had failed in his task. And the seed heads were gone.

"They weren't even mature," mourned Miss Plowright. "They weren't ripe, and now the seeds won't germinate. He won't get any good out of them—whoever he is."

"I didn't tell anybody. I never even said the name." Jeff wished he were dead and underground. Miss Plowright looked at him sadly. He couldn't bear the look in her eyes. Perhaps she believed he had taken them? Had sold them?

"I'm sure you didn't," she said. "The fact that someone knew where they were need not be your fault at all. These things get around."

"It's my fault they were stolen," said Jeff. "*I* fell asleep." Wretchedly he stared back at Miss Plowright, with eyes full of tears. And she had no comfort to offer him.

* * *

"She did offer me the pay, but of course I wouldn't take it," he told Aunt Jean later.

"*Course* you couldn't," croaked Sim, who, mercifully, was a little better that morning, off the oxygen and even able to drink some orange juice from a cup.

Then Sim added thoughtfully, "I'm going to put Great-great-great-Grandma's curse on whoever took the monkey orchid. Maybe that'll protect all the other specimens too."

"Don't try to talk, child, you'll tire yourself," warned Aunt Jean, carrying a bowl and towel out of the room. But Jeff could see that the idea of the curse was a distraction from his own misery and discomfort.

Sim went on slowly, "I bet if Great-Granny Elspeth had been in charge of the orchids, she'd have set a guardian by them."

"What sort of guardian?" asked Jeff, humoring him.

"Like a great black shaggy monkey—but shapeless and soggy, with cold arms, ice-cold hands and feet that would grab you and hold you tight to its soggy chest. And it would puff into your face with its cold stinking breath—like the smell from a garbage can. It would feel like all the hate in the world, come to grab you: hate that's been piling up for hundreds of years."

"Don't!" said Jeff with a shiver. Sim's words somehow embodied the very thought he had had in his own mind; he could feel the awful black thing take shape and expand, like a heaving black balloon, out there, or in there—

To distract himself from the thought he said, "I'm sorry, I'm really sorry about Niagara, Simmie."

"Oh, that's all right. Niagara doesn't matter a bit," Sim said absently. "I don't suppose I'd have been able to draw it, anyway. Why don't you collect me a lot of those beer-can tops, the ones with loops and rings? I've got an awfully good idea for making a pattern."

Mr. Goodman was extremely shocked when he heard, after Jeff had gone back to work, that the two hundred and forty pounds had not been paid and the Niagara trip was off.

"No! Well I never! What a blessed shame! I'm *surprised* at those people. After all, you did the watching, quite okay, for two and half weeks, you ought to have been paid for *that.* They might at least have paid you two hundred—or two twenty." He seemed really outraged, and paid no heed when Jeff said he wouldn't have accepted the money anyway. "I hate for that poor mite of a lad to be disappointed, when he's got nothing else to look forward to."

Mr. Goodman worked for a while in silence, sorting invoices. He seemed to be turning Sim's condition over in his mind, perhaps comparing it to his own—today, for some reason, he seemed particularly pink and pleased with himself. He said, "Business isn't bad, I've had one or two strokes of luck lately, maybe I could see my way to a bit of a donation—"

Jeff stared at him in horror. He muttered, "Oh, no, that wouldn't—" and then found he couldn't bear to stay in Mr. Goodman's presence a moment longer. There was something about those pink cheeks, those bright little eyes, those big clever fingers so handy with pliers or screwdriver, that made him feel sick. He bolted out saying something about a thermostat.

But late that evening, when Jeff arrived home through thundery rain, he found Mr. Goodman there already with Aunt Jean, making his offer. "I'll be only too glad to pay the lad's fare, if that's what he's set his heart on. In fact I've a check already written—"

"But it's not what I've set my heart on, Mr. Goodman," whispered Sim. "I don't feel quite up to drawing Niagara. Instead I'm planning a picture of my great-great-great-grandmother's curse. D'you want to hear about it, Mr. Goodman? She put it on the people who did her harm. It looks like a gathering—a great poisoned swelling in the shape of a monkey that will grow inside a person, inside the thief who stole the flowers that Jeff was looking after. Soon, very soon, it will burst out of that person, like the seed out of a pod—"

"Don't, Sim!" cried out Jeff. "You mustn't!"

But Mr. Goodman, without waiting for Sim to finish, had run out of the room and out of the house. A jag of lightning greeted him, and a flurry of rain: summer was breaking up fast.

"What in the world ails the man?" demanded Aunt Jean, coming in with a cup of milk. "Was he taken ill? He looked terrible."

"He's afraid of illness," Sim said calmly. "Did you remember to bring me any beer-can tops, Jeff?"

"I did find half a dozen." Jeff looked dazed. Slowly he emptied his pockets. "Here. . . ." He was thinking about the monkey: the black, wet, heavy, hating monkey. Gradually, by slow degrees, it lifted itself away from him and drifted away, after Mr. Goodman, into the outside world. Let it go! Let it never come back! "Here they are," he said, and arranged the can tops on Sim's bedside table.

Sim, still too weak to make a drawing of them, lay back on his pillow and looked them over with great content.

"They'll do nicely," he said.

The two brothers rested in silence until Sim sighed and murmured, "Say Chidiock's poem. Say it all through."

> "My prime of youth is but a frost of cares
> My feast of joy is but a dish of pain
> My crop of corn is but a field of tares
> And all my good is but vain hope of gain.
> The day is past and yet I saw no sun
> And now I live and now my life is done."

Jeff said the other two verses as well.

"It's very good," Sim mumbled. "Listen to how those words plod along, like a slow march. Like a person walking through mud. But you'll write one as good, by and by. Did you finish the one you were working on last night?"

"No. I stuck on a rhyme for silver."

"You'll finish it sometime," said Sim.

Jeff was out of a job, after Mr. Goodman's unexpected death, but Miss Plowright offered him one.

"Would you trust me?" he said.

"Of course I would! I could see how dreadfully upset you were about those seeds. And there are lots of things you can do for us if you care to learn a bit about plants. Perhaps you could go to evening classes."

"I'd like to do that," said Jeff. "Later."

Miss Plowright, who had come to the Tichbornes' house, understood him perfectly.

"Of course, later. I believe your brother is handy with wild creatures? I've got a hedgehog here that was found on the Canterbury road—we've mended its leg, but it needs a place to convalesce for a few days. Do you think—your garden—?"

Sim smiled gently at Miss Plowright. They seemed to have made friends without even having exchanged a single word.

The Ill-Natured
Muse

When the desk arrived at his little house in Seymour Mews, Fred Rochester was on the point of going out. His swiftly knotted tie was impeccable, his discreetly cut dark suit would have done credit to a diplomat; his face and hair were respectively impassive and smooth, except for the black lock which curved in a semicolon over his brow and made susceptible young ladies occasionally mistake him for James Bond.

He paused on the step to check his latchkey, and it was at this moment that the van pulled up beside him. It was an elderly, battered vehicle which looked as if it might have come a long, long way; the words A. HOLE & SON, HAULAGE & REMOVALS appeared in trailing letters along the side of the cab, out of which a bent and wizened little man, frail as a dried leaf, deftly sprang.

This individual ran a thumb down a grubby consignment list, nodding familiarly to Frederick.

"That's the one, I thank you, sir," he said, as if continuing some previous conversation. "Number thirteen here, antic desk, Just sign and I'll take her in for you."

"What the devil are you talking about?" inquired Fred, but quite amiably. "You have come to the wrong house; I haven't ordered any furniture."

"Name's Rochester, ent it, sir? That's what it says here. J. W. Rochester, Helicon Cottage, Seymour Mews. Yes, sir, that's your desk all right and tight. We been a long time on the way but we got here in the end."

"There must be some mistake," Fred repeated calmly. "I suggest you ring your boss."

"I *am* the boss." The little man gave an eldritch chuckle.

"Mr. Hole?"

"Properly speaking," the little man confided, "Mr. Hole's me granfer. They calls me dad Half-Hole and me, I'm Quarter-Hole, but me granfer's retired, and me dad only takes on the long-distance jobs. I'm the working partner, so to say. This consignment's all correct, you can take my word, sir."

"But where does it come from?"

"Ah, couldn't say, sir. But it's your address, right enough, ennit?"

"Let's have a look at the desk," Rochester conceded, and Mr. Hole skipped round to the back of the van and pushed aside the dingy old curtain of sacking which protected the interior. Rochester noticed a large bird-cage, a lion skin, a harp (sadly in want of repair), a stuffed crocodile, and a spinning wheel. In front of these articles stood the desk, lashed precariously to the crocodile by a length of cord.

"Lovely bit o' work," said Mr. Hole, rubbing a caressing thumb down one of the bulbous dusty legs. "Jacobean this is, genuine. Three hundred year if it's a day."

"I can see that," Rochester agreed distastefully. "Not my favorite period for English furniture. However—I daresay the desk has its uses. Thank you, you may take it in. Do you want any help?"

"No thanks, guvnor. She lifts out sweet as a pullet's egg." And, sure enough, frail though he seemed, Mr. Hole whisked out the heavy desk almost before the sentence was completed. "Where d'you want her, sir? This yer study? Right-o." He nimbled the desk through a doorway and planted it in the middle of the carpet. "Fills up the room nicely, dunnit? And now if you'll sign, sir—" He twitched a quill pen from behind his ear and, opening a hidden compartment in the desk, which he treated as familiarly as if he had known it all his life, produced a silver inkstand and sandcaster. He dipped the pen and held it out to Rochester, who signed automatically. "I thank you, master—no, nothing to pay. And I bid you good day."

Mr. Hole took himself off with speed: the van was out of sight before Rochester reached the front door for the second time.

On the step he found his way barred once more by a plump man with a self-satisfied expression who raised a detaining hand. "Are you the householder, sir?"

"Yes, I am, and I've already been detained once and I'm late for an appointment," Rochester snapped.

"Only to ask, sir—I need not inquire if you have a refrigerator, for it goes without saying in this area—but, does it work satisfactorily, sir? Does it freeze as it should? Are you sure, sir, that it entirely fulfills your requirements?"

"Entirely," said Rochester, and the most efficient refrigerator in the world could not have lowered the chill in his tone.

"May I inquire, sir, do you use your refrigerator more for, say, sorbet or iced lager?"

"If you must know," snarled Rochester, "I am a dipsomaniac safe-blower, and I keep my perfectly adequate fridge stocked entirely with tequila and my own brand of jellied gelignite. I'm on my way to blow a safe now, and, thanks to you, I'm behind schedule and the jelly is beginning to melt."

"Quite a sense of humor, sir," the plump man replied indulgently. "Well, if you are suited I won't trouble you further at present, but always remember if you are ever dissatisfied you have only to call ColdCo Refrigeration, and we shall be glad to help you."

"Thanks," Rochester said, mechanically pocketing the card which the salesman handed him. As he drove away he noticed with faint disquiet that the man was still gazing after him.

Rochester had been truthful in asserting that he was a safe blower, though the admission had been startled out of him by irritation, and was not one he customarily made. In fact he passed for a man-about-town, an elegant skater on society's surface, and, in the intervals of crib cracking, spent his time at coming-out dances, first nights, private views, and select parties, where, besides diverting himself, he often obtained information that materially helped him in his professional activities. His engagement book would have interested Scotland Yard, for it was layered with such entries as:

June 9.   11 P.M. Drinks at Hot Spot with Sarah
          Somerset
          11.45 Chubb safe Egerton Crescent
          12.00 Hot dogs on Embankment with
          Reeves

Rochester was now on his way to a house called Pelletts, some forty miles the other side of London. It belonged to Sir Gabriel Fidd and its name was a reminder that the vast Fidd fortune had come from the chickenfeed business. Rochester had reason to know that the Fidds were spending the weekend at Montfidget and that Lady Fidd had left her fabulous necklace of condor's-blood rubies at home, "because," she had confided at a dinner party two nights ago, "sea air always makes them look utterly dim and cheesy."

The house was shut, bolted, and barred; the staff were out at a disco affair in the village three miles away. Frederick calmly parked in the stable yard and cut a neat hole in the back door with a thousand-rev-a-minute battery-operated drill.

He walked up the back stairs to the library, where the safe was concealed behind a dummy shelf of calfbound classics.

Unhurrying, working with the pleasurable absorption of the craftsman, he propped open the dummy shelf, built a neat little fosse of plastic putty in front of the safe, pulled a tube out of his pocket, and proceeded to squeeze from it into the crack round the door a quantity of slimy yellow paste.

"What's that jelly?" asked a voice over his shoulder.

With admirable presence of mind Rochester let his back and shoulders absorb the shock of this interruption;

9 3

his rubber-gloved hands remained steady at their task, and he turned his head slowly to look at the yellow-haired girl who was standing behind him interestedly watching the operation.

"What are you doing here?" he said severely. "You are supposed to be at Montfidget."

"I got so bored with the stuffy old duke and duchess that I pretended to have a headache and borrowed Tommy Montfidget's Porsche and drove back to go to the disco; I'm in love with our butler," she candidly replied.

Deborah Fidd was the world's nitwit, but she was undeniably pretty with blond Saxon hair and dark Slav eyes inherited from a Latvian grandmother.

Rochester considered her in perplexed annoyance; according to his usual routine he was now obliged either to shoot or seduce her, but he felt an odd reluctance for either course.

"You haven't answered my question," Deb persisted. "Who are you? And what is that stuff?"

"It's gelignite and I'm about to blow the safe," Rochester said irritably. "Come on, we'd better sit behind the sofa."

Deb giggled. "*That* old gag," she said. "You don't expect—"

Rochester picked her up and deposited her with a bump upon the Aubusson behind a hideous satin-covered but heavy piece of furniture. Next moment there was another soft bump and a small cloud of dust rose.

"Oo! Look what a hole it's made!"

"That was the intention."

"But who are you? I ought to know you but I'm so

hopeless at faces. Omar Sharif is the only one I'm really sure of."

Rochester's hand, in the act of pulling out his Volksluger, hesitated, and came out instead with a small piece of pasteboard.

"I'm from the ColdCo Refrigeration Works," he said. "Your father has been having a spot of bother with his safe, and I've come to fix it for him."

"Do fridge people fix safes? How fascinating."

"Oh, yes, it's always done. When you're grown up and have a safe of your own, if you are ever dissatisfied or need advice, you have only to call ColdCo and we shall be glad to help you."

"Sweet of you, but I'm grown up now. I'm seventeen." She slipped the card absently into the pocket of her maroon velvet pants. "I say, there are Mum's rubies. Aren't they foul? Just like underdone kidneys. I say, have you finished your job now? You wouldn't like to come to the disco with me? Quite honestly you're even handsomer than our butler and it would be rather a thing to make him jealous."

"Sorry, my dear," Rochester said hastily. "That's out of the question."

"Why?"

"Because—because my old aunt's waiting up for me at home."

"I don't believe you've *got* an old aunt," she said crossly. "Anyway, call me next week."

He looked again at the yellow hair and dark-fringed eyes. He melted. "All right," he said with a resigned shrug at his own folly. "And now you'd better run or you'll miss the best part of the party."

He slipped a sheet of paper into Sir Gabriel's secretary's typewriter, rapidly typed on it: *They look like underdone kidneys but you should take better care of these rubies,* and laid it on the necklace.

"Aren't you going to clear up the mess?"

"My mate will do it tomorrow. The union's complaining about my overtime as it is."

He waved her a brisk good-bye and drove roaring back to London wondering what had come over him.

Three A.M. was an odd time to see a light in his front window. Burglars?

He snugged the Volksluger into his right hand as he opened the front door with his left. An elderly lady came out of the study to greet him. "Ah, dear boy, *there* you are! What sadly late hours you keep! This must be remedied."

"And who might you be, madam?" Rochester asked courteously, after one lightning glance round to make sure she was not the extraordinary mouthpiece of cops, strong-arm boys, or foreign intelligence operatives.

Then he remembered his mendacious excuse to Deb. This old dame might have sat as a model for anyone's aunt: she had gray hair, frizzed into a sort of Grecian knot at the back of her head; a round face; and screwed-up eyes peering at him intensely through a formidable pair of sculpted and brilliant-encrusted spectacles; she carried a large knitting bag; the total effect was a potent mixture of good humor and willpower.

"My name," she said, "is Laodameia," and waited for his reaction.

It was nil. "Look," he said, "I'm delighted to meet you but I'm tired just now; I've been out on a job; and I'm sure *you're* wanting to get home; can I drop you anywhere?"

"This is my home," she said.

"Eh?"

"Do you not recognize me, dear boy? I am your Muse. I came with the desk, from now on forevermore to be your Inspiration, your Egeria, your Solace in time of Woe, your Spur, your Stimulus—"

"There must be some mistake," Fred said distinctly. "I'm not a writer."

"You will be from now on, dear boy."

"But I've no use for a Muse! I'm in no need of any spur, stimulus, solace, or what-have-you. Hell!" he burst out indignantly. "What sort of life is it if in his own home a man is pestered with unwanted desks, refrigerators, and now a Muse, of all things?"

"What are you Making of your Life?" asked Laodameia, who tended to speak in capitals. She fixed him with a severe eye. "You have already frittered away your most Prolifick years. From now on, you must work; you must scorn delights and live laborious days. I shall be ever present to raise your Spirit."

She rummaged in a drawer of the desk, brought out a sheet of foolscap paper, and handed him a pen, ready dipped in ink. "Poet, take your lute!" she declaimed.

But Fred had thought of a different kind of spirit. Tequila seemed the only antidote to this overbearing mentor. "Your very good health, ma'am," he said, raising a ten-finger salute, and he downed the lot, his parting thought as he blacked out in rose-red mists being a faint query as to whether it was uncivil not to have offered some to the Muse.

When he woke he remembered the rubies. Where had he stowed them? Then he recalled that for some bird-witted reason he had left them behind. That brought Deb to mind—banana haired, dark eyed, she drifted across his hangover like a salamander through smog.

Last and least probable he remember the Muse. She appeared now like a bad dream, perhaps a retroactive result of the tequila. With cautious optimism he raised himself to drink the black coffee which his char brought him.

"There isn't a strange lady about the house, is there, Mrs. Wappitt?"

The char gave him a startled glance. One for a lark, Mr. Fred was, quite a Don Lothario, but never yet so foolish as to bring a young lady home; he always kept them at the end of their tether.

"I should hope not, sir! I've dusted the new desk, Mr. Fred, and will you be wanting the piano tuner?"

The piano tuner, Reeves, was Rochester's fence, who collected little caches of jewels from inside the Broadwood and disposed of them on the Continent while ostensibly taking orders for cheap British pianos.

"Not today, thanks. Lord, my head!" Rochester groaned, and tottered off to his bath. On the way back he looked into the study. There sat the Muse, immersed in *The Times*. "I invariably peruse all the papers and two new books every day," she said, observing him over her glasses. "So should you. Come now, to work!"

"Mrs. Thing!" bawled Fred. "Show this lady out! Madam," he said to her, "I am unable to comply with your requirements."

Mrs. Wappitt stuck a puzzled face round the door. "You seeing things, Mr. Fred?" she said. "Your head *must* be bad. Try a raw egg in Wooss."

"Hence with denial vain and coy excuse," commanded Laodameia. "I am only visible when I so Chuse —or to those of a Higher Perception. Poet, take your lute."

"How many times do I have to tell you that I don't *have* a lute?" poor Fred snarled, but it was no use; in double-quick time she had him seated at the desk before a thick stack of foolscap, on the topmost page of which she had inscribed in an elaborate seventeenth-century hand:

PHILEMON: A LAMENT IN LXVIII CANTOS
On the Follies and Excefses of
    the Prefent Age

"Begin, and somewhat loudly sweep the string," she ordered. And despite Fred's objection that he didn't in the least want to lament loudly for Philemon, whoever Philemon was, she began dictating at a great rate. He had no course but to take down her words. Soon his hand was aching with the effort to keep pace; hitherto he had hardly written anything longer than a note of acceptance, but the Muse had no mercy on him; they worked steadily through the day and by the time Frederick was allowed to stagger off to bed, more than one hundred and forty-eight pages of foolscap had been covered with iambic pentameters.

Next day saw a repetition of this routine, until eight in the evening, when a duchess called Winnie rang up and invited Fred to an impromptu champagne supper.

"I have to go out now," he told Laodameia.

"Impossible! There are yet twenty-nine cantos to be inscribed."

"I'm afraid social duty calls."

"You fpeak of focial Duty when the Muse dictates?" said she with curling lip. "And what am I to do, pray?"

"Go to bed, sweet Muse," suggested Fred lightheartedly, and escaped.

Alas, whom should he encounter at the party but Deb Fidd, looking silly but ravishing in zebra-striped silk. "Oo, it's my lovely ColdCo man!" she cried, and made a beeline for him. "Do you know, Daddy *hadn't* been expecting you that night, and he was quite cross. He's on the board of ColdCo, and he said nothing of the kind had been arranged. So have they sacked you?"

Evidently Deb's memory for faces was better than she imagined.

"Ah, you must have met my twin brother," Rochester said hastily. "We never speak of him—he's the family black sheep. Look, shall we run away from here and go somewhere amusing?"

Deb was delighted, and he took her to a nightclub called the Custard Apple and made himself so agreeable that he had soon ousted the butler from her fickle heart. He dropped her at her aunt's in Lowndes Square and went on to a little job at a house in Gerrard's Cross which yielded a diamond sunburst, some fair-to-middling pearls, and a box of negotiable securities. Then home to Helicon Cottage where the Muse, who never seemed to tire, was furiously reading *Ulysses*. "Hokey pokey, penny a lump," she muttered. "What means this sorry drivel?"

"I see my Muse labors," remarked Fred, patting her kindly on the shoulder, and he quickly downed a tot of tequila and went to bed before she could think of a rejoinder. But she made him suffer for this next day by indulging in an ostentatious migraine. Her brow wreathed in a damp purple towel, she dictated three cantos, punctuating the lines with heavy sighs.

"The sound is forc'd, the notes are few," she lamented, breaking off. Fred offered aspirin, but she haughtily declined, preferring to gloom about the house in Dolefull Dreariment. Later, however, he found that she had been helping herself lavishly to bread and peanut butter (evidently this delicacy was unknown to her) and he felt less guilty at having caused her headache. Nevertheless, conscience obliged him to stay in that evening instead of going to a film premiere, and she brightened up enough to dictate three more cantos.

After a few days Fred grew more or less resigned to having the Muse about. She seldom slept, but, given plenty of reading matter and a sufficient supply of peanut butter, she would sometimes consent to his taking an hour or two off.

"Just to acquire material," he pleaded.

The Muse was heard to mutter something about ignoble haunts, but she let him go; unfortunately she soon developed a tendency, if he was late, to come and fetch him from whatever party he happened to be gracing. To some she was visible; others remained unaware of her presence. Fred's acquaintances were understandably derisive at the sight of a large cross lady in a purple scarf who hovered like a thunderous nanny on the corners of festive gatherings until she could pounce on her charge and drag him away.

"Of course it's heaven to meet your aunt," a young countess said tactfully at a hilarious session of the Gulliver Club, "but don't you think this is rather the wrong age group for her?"

"You are making me conspicuous," Fred said peevishly to Laodameia; he did not mention his particular reason for finding this undesirable. "Can't you stay home and do the pools or something?"

"Pool, sir? Pool—aye, kennel, puddle, sink!"

"No, dear, football pools." He showed her how, and she developed a surprising aptitude, winning a hundred and twenty pounds the first week, seldom falling short of this figure thereafter. Delighted, Fred took out a subscription to the *Competitors' Monthly,* and began to spend more time away from home, leaving Laodameia at work on verses in praise of peanut butter which, if she won, would entitle her to free supplies of this commodity for life.

When she displayed to Fred her final achievement—

> My song were faint without it; how to utter
> Sufficient praise of Watkyns' peanut butter?

—Fred was a little dubious, feeling the makers would prefer something with more snap, but, not wishing to discourage the old lady, he posted it off.

Relations did not continue long in this amicable train. The couple were at work on Canto XLV that evening when the doorbell rang. Laodameia sniffed, suspicious as a bloodhound, when Fred went to the door.

Deb Fidd blew in like a drift of cherry blossoms.

"Surprise, surprise!" she caroled, giving Fred a spiky potted cactus with a pink flower, and standing on tiptoe to kiss his chin. "Algy Devlin told me where you lived; come on, let's go out and have fun!"

Casting a guilty glance toward the study, where Laodameia, at sight of the visitor, had begun swelling with doom-laden reproach, Rochester grabbed his car key and left.

When he arrived home at four A.M., having gleaned a very good tiara in Cadogan Square on the way back, he was subjected to a torrent of reproach and accusations of frivolous living. The Muse quoted some vindictive remarks about painted faces in Hyde Park by Thomas Randolph and ended significantly, "My *Muse* were she my Love should be."

"Let's discuss it tomorrow, shall we?" begged Fred sleepily, gulping tequila as she shut the tiara into the piano.

"I will call you betimes," said she with ominous brow.

"I'm taking Deb to Wimbledon; shan't be home till five." He was instantly asleep.

The Muse retired to brood over the glossy magazines and the collected plays of G. B. Shaw. She rummaged the fridge for peanut butter and, finding the supply exhausted, fell back on playing the piano. Her choice of music was funereal, but fortunately it was audible only to Fred.

At seven he staggered up, despairing of sleep. "For heaven's sake, put away that tiara!" he snapped. She had perched it rakishly atop of her purple turban.

"I misdoubt it was not Come by Honestly," she reproved him.

"I'll thank you to remember that my morals at least are my own affair."

With an ill grace he scribbled down half a dozen stanzas. Then he bathed, shaved, and left the thankless Muse for the more attractive company of Deb. Laodameia watched his departure with a kindling eye, then sat down to study the morning paper, which carried a headline story about the theft of Lady Inkwell's jewels, with a picture of the tiara inset.

By the end of the morning, despite interruptions from the char and piano tuner, Laodameia had absorbed enough information to telephone Scotland Yard. Her statement corroborated evidence already collected by a plainclothesman masquerading as a refrigerator salesman, and was received with gratifying interest.

When Rochester came home that evening the Muse was all smiles, even when he warned her that he would shortly be going out again.

"A cheerful life is what the Mufes love," she remarked surprisingly. "Come: let us fit upon the rocks and fee the fhepherds feed their flocks."

"Perhaps tomorrow?" Frederick said cautiously.

"I fpake in metaphor. I will Accompanie you to the busie haunts of men."

"I'm going out on a job," he replied, taking tubes of his patent mixture from the fridge.

"The man who weds the facred Mufe, Disdains all mercenary views," she countered.

"Who pays for the peanut butter? Unless you win a lifetime supply, we need cash to eat. I'm off to crack a safe in Aylesbury."

"I know," replied the Muse, who had been studying his engagement calendar.

The motor trip to Berkshire upset her vibrations and she disappeared, but materialized beside him as he began operations on the safe, which belonged to the marchioness of Tring. Laodameia watched for a few minutes as he dibbled in his explosive, then, to his dismay, she began declaiming verse at the top of her lungs:

> The Muse has broke the twilight's gloom
> To cheer the shiv'ring native's dull
>   abode. . . .
> Her track, where'er the Goddess roves
> Glory pursue, and generous Shame
> Th'unconquerable Mind, and Freedom's
>   holy flame!

"Will you be *quiet*!" exclaimed the scandalized Fred. "I'd never have let you come along if I'd known you'd kick up such a row—"

Her words had been a signal, however, and twenty police burst into the room. Fred could see the game was up; he made no attempt to resist arrest, but had the presence of mind to drop his Volksluger into the Muse's knitting bag. She stood loftily apart and took no further hand in the proceedings. Indeed the CID men, who must have been lacking in Higher Perception, remained oblivious of her presence, and were rather puzzled as to who had given the signal. This fact remained a mystery throughout the trial, which was a society sensation. Deb Fidd weepingly testified to the beauty of Fred's character and added that she was engaged to him—which her father contradicted—but her unsupported testimony was not enough to counteract the effect of the flagrante delicto capture and the jelly found in the fridge. Fred received a stiff sentence; his one consolation being that Laodameia, after the betrayal, had at least seen fit to disappear and leave him in decent solitude.

Deb managed an interview with him before he was taken away.

"I'll wait for you!" she cried tearfully. "I'll send you a file in a pie!"

He hugged her and whispered, "Not a file, ninny—skeleton keys!"

But several months elapsed before he heard from her again and meanwhile, to his utter horror, the Muse suddenly reappeared and took up most unwelcome residence in his cell. Vainly he pleaded the impropriety of this.

"What Bard could wish a more secluded spot; nor mossie Dell, nor Grove, nor Fernie Grot?" she observed, and began to dictate Canto XLVI.

"*O Muse, spectre insatiable!*" grumbled Rochester, who could quote too. "*Ne m'en demande pas si long!*" and he added, "I'm surprised you have the effrontery to show your face here."

"But, dear boy, it was for the Advancement of Literature that I brought you to this peaceful place."

Fred was digesting this when the warder poked his head in. "Letter for you, mate, and a tube of hand cream from your girlfriend."

Deb's letter was very short. "Darling Fred, this is to say Good-bye. I fear you will say I have a very ficcle nature, but am going to marry Tommy Montfidget so have to break off our engagement. Will send skel key when back from honeymoon. Tons of love, Deb."

Laodameia scanned the envelope with a puzzled frown. "Young man—" she said.

But it took her some time to attract Fred's attention. Lovely Deb, darling Deb—like thistledown she had drifted into his life and out of it again. Kissing her hand in an airy good-bye she drifted away. . . .

"I—I beg your pardon, did you speak?" he said to the Muse.

"Why is that envelope addressed to Frederick Rochester?"

"That's my name."

"Not John Wilmot, earl of Rochester?"

"Certainly not."

"1980!" she said, staring at the postmark. "Not 1680!"

"Dear me, no."

"Alack!" she cried. "Too late! Oh, woe is me! I am undone. I must be gone."

Gathering up her knitting she gave Fred an absent farewell pat on the head and disappeared without more ado. Mechanically Rochester put the tube of jelly into his sponge bag and sat down to savor his new-found freedom. No Muse is good news—or so many a harassed poet has claimed; but now the old baggage was gone he quite found that he missed her, and would have been glad to see her back.

"Your birthday or something?" asked the warder, poking in another letter that evening.

Dear Sir,

We are pleased to inform you that your entry, received together with twenty labels from Watkyns' peanut butter jars, has been adjudged winner of our competition by a panel of Expert Judges. This is to instruct you that we are prepared to send you a weekly supply, free, for the rest of your natural life, of Watkyns' superfine

107

peanut butter. Could you inform us whether you would prefer Crunchy or Smooth . . . ?

How Laodameia would enjoy it, he thought.
Perhaps if I work hard at my writing, she might come back.
Doggedly he sat down, wrapped a damp sock round his brow, licked the stub of pencil the prison allowed him, and started work on Canto XLVII:

> Art must knit up the ravel'd Sock of Life
> The Poet woos the Muse before the
> Wife. . . .

The Erl King's Daughter

These things happened to my younger brother Kevin when I was in the hospital. If I'd not been in the hospital, maybe I could have helped him.

It was after Gran died. Gran and me got hit by a truck whose brakes failed, coming down Squires Hill. It ran up on the pavement. Gran was killed and I had a busted leg; it was busted in two places, so that took weeks to mend. Up to then, Gran was looking after me and Kev, because our dad died years ago. And Mum does a lot of competition dancing with her friend Mr. Chepstow, so she's mostly away. When she is home, she's busy making her fancy costumes, or mending them.

After Gran got killed, Aunt Ada, that's Mum's sister, came to look after Kev, and, if you ask me, Aunt Ada's no more use than last week's paper. She's thin, and forgets everything you tell her; she has a whiny voice and a drip on the end of her nose.

Well. Just after I got my leg busted, a new girl turned up in Kev's class at our school, that's Kimballs Green Middle School. Her name was Nora Scull. Kev told me about Nora when Aunt Ada brought him to visit me at Squires Park Hospital.

Kev has a knack for telling stories. He got that from our gran. She came from abroad, when she was little, with *her* gran, who knew lots of tales about trolls and kobolds and witches. Our gran passed these on to Kev, and he told them to the kids at school.

Kev is little and pale and scrawny, he can't run fast, for he gets out of breath, so he does more watching and thinking than most people, and knows a lot of words. He reads all the labels on packets and he can tell stories pretty well. Better than I can; I always seem to get the back bits in the front. And forget the middle bits.

When he came to see me at the hospital, Kev told me what this Nora looked like. She was put in his class, though she was older, because she never had much schooling; her dad was always on the move. She was skinny as a broom, Kev told me, with eyes black as lumps of soot, and a sharp nose. Her hair was dark and thick, so thick and bushy that she always seemed to be hidden behind it, in a dark corner of her own. She never laughed, never smiled, never got angry or miserable. Just watched and watched, all the time. Rather like Kev, in a way.

Right from the start, Nora latched on to Kev. Took a strong fancy to him. I asked him why. He couldn't say. She was older and bigger, you'd think she'd want to be with those of her own age. But no, she always made for Kev. Maybe it was because of his tales. Though, he said, if he did tell one, she'd sneer at it, and find fault, and say it was a silly baby story.

Only one she ever liked, and that was the story of the Erl King.

The Erl King's Daughter

That was one our gran used to tell about the forests in the land *her* gran came from. In those big woods there lives a spook, and his name's the Erl King. He rides about at night, on his big black horse that goes like the wind, but completely quiet, you can't hear it. And there was a farmer had to go through the woods one night, taking his baby son, who's sick, to the doctor.

The man carries the sick kid on his back, in a carrier, and the kid keeps crying, and saying, "Dada, Dada, the Erl King's chasing us, he's grabbing at me with his cold bony hands." Well, the father runs faster and faster, to get away from the Erl King, but it's no use. When he gets to where the doctor lives, he *thinks* he's saved his son, but the little kid is stone cold dead in his carry bag.

So the Erl King did get him after all.

Gran used to tell us that story, once in a way, and then Kev told it to the others in his class. When Kev used to tell it, he changed it a bit. Instead of those foreign woods, he had the father running along the public footpath that's the old, disused railway between Turnpike Heath and Squires Park Hospital. There's a big patch of copse wood on Turnpike Heath, comes right down to the railway cutting, and after Kev had told the story once or twice, some of the kids wouldn't go near those woods or the railway path. They said the Erl King would get them.

Nora really took a liking to that story, Kev said. And, after she'd made him tell it once or twice, *she* got to telling it herself, and she made it ever so much more scary each time, putting in awful things, about the Erl King, and how he followed the father through Kimballs Green Cemetery, and across the Sports Ground, and up

Squires Hill—and then, just as the father gets to the hospital forecourt, the ghost makes his last wicked grab.

"Do you *like* Nora?" I asked Kev.

"No," he said. "No, I don't like her."

Kev himself just about stopped telling stories at this time.

I only found that out later. But I could see there was something wrong with him, when Aunt Ada brought him visiting at the hospital, for he'd got so thin and waxy pale, with eyes as big as olives and dark-gray hollows under them. But then, of course, I thought it was from grieving for our gran. He did grieve for her a lot. Kev and Gran were always very close. As well as telling him tales, she used to let him help her about the house, before he started school, and in the kitchen. They'd talk and chatter to each other all day long. She had lots of ideas about things, did our gran. Anything from people to potatoes. So it was only to be expected he'd miss her badly.

Gran was a champion cook too. Not fancy stuff— she'd no time or cash for that—but things you don't get in other kids' places: onion-and-raw-potato pancakes, gingerbread, cheese pudding, home-baked beans.

After Aunt Ada moved in, it was all frozen stuff. "I'm no cook, never have been," she'd say, sniffing. "I've taken on the care of two children, all that extra trouble at my age, can't expect me to cook as well." It was fish fingers and peas day after day, Kev told me.

And, do you know what Aunt Ada *did*— she got rid of all Gran's things. Every bit. Her clothes went to the jumble; and her little old clock, her brass pot and meat-pounder, her curved chopper and wooden spoons and big wooden bowl, were sold to Mr. Simms, who has the secondhand shop on Turnpike Hill.

And—worst of all for Kev—he found that her little cookery book had gone too. It wasn't very big, not much bigger than a packet of crisp-bread, with a flaking back and a thick old rubber band round, because of all the bits and pieces that were tucked into it. *The Working Lady's Cook-Book*, it was called. Gran had it from her mum, and both of them had written notes in the margins, and drawn little pictures, to show how things ought to be cut or peeled or shaped, and had stuck in bits out of newspapers and magazines, till the book was more like a family scrapbook than a cookery book. There were as many handwritten lines as printed ones.

When Kev got home from school one day and found the book missing from the shelf where the salt, pepper, and mustard are kept, he was really upset. He asked Aunt Ada where it was. "I disposed of it," she says. "Best you got nothing to remind you of your gran. You fret for her too much as it is."

"What did you do with the book?" says Kev.

"Never you mind. It's none of your affair. What d'you want with a cookery book, anyway? Cooking is girls' business."

Kev couldn't get any more out of Aunt Ada. He did go and ask Mr. Simms, but the book wasn't in the junk shop with the brass pot and the other things. Kev was terribly afraid that Aunt Ada had just put it in the trash.

He looked there, too, but he didn't find it.

That was a bad time for Kev, and the new girl at school, Nora Scull, she made things worse.

She was always following Kev around. "Softy," she called him, or "Dummy."

One day he saw Miss Clamp's brooch lying in the playground, and picked it up. Nora pounced on him and snatched it.

"You give me that, Softy!"

"It's Miss Clamp's!"

"Give it here!"

"It's not yours."

"If you don't hand it over, I'll put such an ache into your head that you won't be able to see the blackboard."

Kev gets these awful headaches now and then. They last for a day, very bad. He has to go home and lie down. Somehow Nora had found out about them.

"I can give you one," she told him, "if I just point my finger at you—like this!" Just the sight of that skinny pointing finger, and her dark eyes, like black holes, made Kev's head begin to throb, like a brass band, a long way off.

"Do you know who I *am*?" she says.

"Yes, you're Nora Scull."

"I'm more than that! I'm the Erl King's daughter. And if you don't do what I say, I shall get my dad to come and fetch you."

Well—Kev believed her. He knew where she lived, down Spital Way, that's a very bad neighborhood. All the houses are due to be pulled down and high-rises built. Kimballs Green is a run-down part of London, and Spital Way, in the middle, is the worst bit. Nora lived in an empty house, in a Squat, with her father. It was all boarded up. Nora climbed in and out every day through a hole over a big rusty tank. Once she tried to get Kev to go in there, but he wouldn't. It was just the kind of place, he thought, where the Erl King would choose to live, with a lot of rusty old gas cookers and smashed TV sets in the front yard.

"Don't you go telling any of the others about my dad being the Erl King," says Nora. "I'll know, right off, if you do. I know every single thing that happens to you. And if you tell *anybody*, my dad will come and get you. He'll come on his black Koniyashi that can go up stairs and in windows."

That really gave Kev the shivers. So when Miss Clamp asked, in assembly, had anyone seen her brooch, he bit his lip and kept quiet. He felt awful about it, though, because he liked Miss Clamp.

None of the other kids could stand Nora, so, as Kev was always in her company, his friends stopped talking to him. He and Nora got left alone together. And she'd follow him home, or up the street, wherever he went. Aunt Ada, at home, didn't mind Nora, because she was quiet. "I don't object to a quiet, well-behaved child," she said. Nora would sit in our front room, with her sharp eyes everywhere, waiting for a chance to whip a chocolate biscuit out of the tin, or a 20p from Aunt Ada's purse. She never took enough to notice, but she was always at it, thieving.

"If you tell on me, I shall say you took it," she told Kev.

There's an old blind man, sits on a box all day outside Kimballs Green tube station. Mr. Greenway, his name is. Lives in Turnpike Lane with his daughter. She won't have him in the house during the day, so he sits on the box with his dog, Spot, on his lap, and a plate in front for coins people drop in. He doesn't get much. And Spot always looks sorry for himself, and a bit embarrassed, sitting on Mr. Greenway's lap like that. He's really too big, and his legs hang down. Still, he puts up with it. He gives his stumpy tail a wag when Kev goes by on the way to school, because sometimes Kev brings him a bone.

One day, walking home past the tube station— "Wouldn't it be a lark to tip Spot into the road?" says Nora.

"No it *wouldn't,*" says Kev.

But next minute Nora gets behind Mr. Greenway on his box and gives him a hard shove; over he goes, sprawling on the pavement, and Spot is thrown clear into the traffic. There's a horrible screech of brakes.

Right away, Nora's picking Mr. Greenway up, making a big fuss of him.

"Oh, you poor old man! I saw those wicked boys knock you over!"

Butter wouldn't melt in her mouth, you'd think. And while she was setting him back on his box, she half-inched 50p out of his scattered money.

Spot came limping back out of the traffic with a hurt leg. "Lucky he wasn't killed," said an angry motorcyclist. "Ooh, those wicked boys," says Nora, rolling up her eyes. "What things are coming to I don't know, I'm sure."

"I'm not going to talk to you anymore," says Kev to Nora afterward. "That was a horrible trick to play."

"If you tell, I'll strike you blind," says Nora. "I can do that, just as easy as give you a headache. How would you like to have to sit on a box for the rest of your life, in the dark, like the old man? I can do it," she says, "if I point my finger at you."

And Kev believed her. When she pointed her finger, everything in front of his eyes began to darken and blur and slip about.

Next, Nora made him go into shops and ask for a thing that might be hard to find—like junket mix, or almond flavoring—and while the shopkeeper was hunting, she'd whip something from a stand near the door, chewing gum or mints or all-sorts. If the shopkeeper did manage to find some junket mix she'd say, "No, that's not the sort our mum wants."

Kev was growing thinner and thinner, he had awful dreams at night, about the Erl King coming to fetch him and shut him up in the dark forever. And his headaches got worse, and came more often.

One day, after school, Nora says to Kev, "Come on, I've found a new place. It's in March Street, down our way. There's a poky old bookshop, and it's run by a dippy old girl who's deaf as a post; we can go in and sneak up behind her and take all the cash out of her drawer."

Kev didn't want to go. He hates that part of Kimballs Green, down near the gasworks and the canal. And he was afraid that Nora's father might come out of the Squat and get him. And he was scared that something bad might happen in the shop.

"I'm going home," he said. "I don't want to come with you."

"I'll make your head ache!" says Nora. "It'll be the worst headache you ever had." And she points her finger at him. Right away, he can feel a thump-thump start up, in back of his eyes.

So he went along with Nora, but very slowly, dragging his feet, keeping several paces behind, and thinking about Gran. If only Gran were still alive, he thought.

117

She wouldn't put up with Nora, not for five minutes. "I don't like craftiness nor malice," she used to say. "And I don't like folk that's out only for theirselves. That sort, you want to keep clear of them. Tell them to clear out. Have nothing to do with them."

"But suppose they won't clear off, Gran, then what?" Kevin asked her once.

And what had Gran said then?

"This is the place," said Nora, and turned into a street of dingy houses that led off Spital Way. The doors opened flat on the pavement, but most were boarded up. One of them was still open, and the front window beside it was full of grimy books.

By now it was October, a foggy evening, cold, beginning to get dark.

Kev had a horrible feeling of danger. He was sure something bad was going to happen when he was in the bookshop.

Only a dim light showed in the window, and the glass was very grimy. But still, Kev could just see through, and he could see shelves all round the small shop, full of books, and a desk in the middle, with more books piled on that, and somebody sitting behind the desk. Kev had never seen a shop full of books before— there's nothing of that kind up where we live, top of Squires Hill—and he couldn't help being interested, in spite of feeling so cold and sick and scared.

But Nora seemed put out. A gray sour look went over her face—like the wind shifting over a bed of nettles. "Blow it," she says sharply, "there's someone new in there. Maybe the old lady got ill. Maybe she died. We'll have to think of another plan. I know: you go in, and start looking about. I'll stay out here, and presently I'll start to shout, 'Help, help!' Then the chap will run out, to see what's happening, and you grab the money that's in the drawer. The old girl always kept it in a green tin cashbox. Hurry up—in you go."

So Kev went into the shop—scared and hollow-feeling, not wanting to go in, yet in spite of himself he couldn't help being keen to see this place full of books.

And another part of him was thinking about Spital Way, just round the corner, where Nora's father the Erl King lived in his dark Squat; and another part was trying to remember what Gran had said, what *had* she said, about bad people and how to deal with them?

Something about darkness, it was.

If only he could remember.

He went slowly into the shop, which smelled of old, musty dusty books. The young man at the desk looked up from something he was studying and gave Kev a half smile.

"Hallo, son. Looking for any book in particular?"

Kev could only answer in a mumble. "Can I—can I have a look round?"

"Feel free."

The young fellow—he was pale, with ginger hair—he went back to his reading. Outside the window, Kev could see Nora's eyes like two black holes, looking in, and her nose pressed against the glass.

Kev stared at the backs of all the books—there were thousands of them, hardbacks and paperbacks—and wondered how long it would take to read them all. Weeks, months. Then he looked at Nora again and saw she was pointing toward the desk where the young man sat, and its drawer. Kev moved a little closer, pretending

JOAN AIKEN

to be studying the books that were on the shelves along by the side of the desk.

Then his eyes nearly dropped out of his head. For there, lying on the desk, open, with all its old bits spread about, and its thick rubber band, was Gran's cookery book. *That* was what the young man was studying so carefully!

Kev let out a kind of a squawk.

"Why!" he said. "That's my gran's cookbook! That's her *cookbook*! I thought Aunt Ada had thrown it away. Did she—did she sell it to you?"

"Not to me," says the young man. "I just took on this place from my auntie Tilly who had a stroke. Was your grandmother's name Martha Green?"

"Yes—*yes*— and all those notes are in her writing— and my great-gran's—"

Kev was so excited he was trembling. And, just at that moment, he remembered part of what Gran had said—about darkness, it was—

The young man seemed quite excited too. "But it's the most wonderful book," he was saying. "I'm going to see if I can't get it published—notes and all—did your gran draw those pictures?"

"Yes, she did—"

"I'm sure I can find a publisher who will want to do it—"

Turn their own darkness against them, Gran had said. They drag their own dark about inside them. Leave them to smash themselves up. They'll do it fast enough. Just you keep clear of them, Kev, my boy, and let them dig their own pit. And then they'll fall into it.

Kev thought of the Erl King, riding through the dark on his motorbike, with his long bony fingers reaching

out, ready to grab. He thought of the black holes of
Nora's eyes.

And, just at that moment, he heard Nora's voice
outside the window.

"Help! *Help! HELP!*"

"God save us, what's *that*?" gasped the young man.
He jumped up, knocking over his chair, and rushed to
the door. Kev forgot his orders to empty the cashbox,
and followed. They both ran into the street.

Now, here's the queer part.

That street was perfectly empty, from end to end.

Not a single soul to be seen. Nora wasn't there. Nor
was anybody else. Though they hunted from end to
end of March Street, from Squires Hill to Kimballs
Green tube.

Nora didn't turn up at school next day. She
wasn't in her seat next to Kev. And he never saw her
again. Soon after that, a demolition firm came and
knocked down the whole row of houses in Spital Way,
where the Erl King had his Squat.

Some of the kids at Kimballs Green Middle aren't
certain if Nora was ever there. Lots don't remember
her.

When my leg was mended I came out of hospital,
and after a while Kev stopped looking so thin and
miserable.

The young man in the bookshop—Alan Hudnut's his
name—has found a publisher who wants to print Gran's
book. The *Survivor's Kitchen Book,* it's going to be
called. And it'll have all Gran's little pictures, and what
she wrote in the front. *This book is for my grandson,*

Kevin Green. That's going to be printed at the beginning. Alan Hudnut thinks Kev ought to get quite a bit of money from the sales of the book, by and by.

Aunt Ada is still thin and whiny, but Kevin and I have taken over the cooking now, so she just sits in the front room and does her crochet. She only got 15p from Alan's auntie Tilly Hudnut for the cookbook, so it was hardly worth her trouble walking all that way down Squires Hill.

Kev's going to be a famous chef when he grows up, he says. He's given up telling stories altogether.

But the queer thing is that the kids at school still tell the story of the Erl King; and lots of them won't go along the old railway path to Squires Park or into Turnpike Woods.

They say the woods are haunted by a witch girl called Nora Scull.

The End
of Silence

It was after Ma died that our father acquired the owl, and we started to hate him.

She was killed by a bomb. It happened at Frankfurt airport, when she was on her way back from a visit to Aunt Ginnie. "Good-bye, see you next Saturday, I've left enough cooked food in the freezer for a week, and I'll try to bring back some German rock records," she said, when she left, six days earlier, and that was the last time we saw her. Death is extremely shattering when it comes baldly and unexpectedly like that; if somebody is ill, or in hospital, you have a little time to adjust, a little time for your mind to prepare. But in such a situation as ours, no way. I know this sounds obvious, but when you yourself are the victim, the truth of it really hits you.

We were all knocked out in different ways. My sister Helen went silent. I began addictively eating tortilla chips and reading murder mysteries. Bag after bag of chips, book after book, two or three a day. I got them from the local library or bought secondhand paperbacks from the Old Bus Station Wholesale Goods Mart. "You'll get horribly fat if you don't stop," Helen broke her silence to say. But I couldn't stop. Reading was a drug that numbed the pain.

Father came out worst. He went silent, too, and lost a couple of stone in weight. Then he suddenly announced that he was sending us to boarding school.

His explanation *sounded* reasonable.

"I'm a writer, damn it! I've got to support us all and keep up the mortgage payments. My inventive faculty has to keep functioning, which is hard enough in present circumstances, Lord knows. How do you think I'd manage if I had to keep remembering about things like fetching you from school and stew for dinner?"

Ma would have managed somehow, if she'd been the one who was left, I thought but didn't say. Helen pressed her lips together and stared at her feet and then turned and walked away.

Apart from the shock of losing all our friends and familiar surroundings at one sweep, the boarding school wasn't too bad. People knew what had happened to us and were kind without making a fuss. Our connection with Father was a help, I suppose. He is fairly well known because, besides being a poet and an expert on Anglo-Saxon, he wrote that book about Alfred and the Danes, *The King's Jewel,* which they did on television and it was very successful.

Which was one reason why we took his excuses for packing us off to boarding school with more than a pinch of salt.

"He just wants to get rid of us," I said, "because we remind him of Ma."

"Well—he does have to look ahead," Helen argued. "One TV success won't last forever. And it's four years since he wrote the *Jewel.* I'm sure he isn't doing any

124

work. He just goes into the study and sits. I've seen him, through the window."

"That's why he doesn't want us at home. He's afraid we'll ask what he's working on."

When we went home for Christmas, there was the owl.

Aunt Joe had given it to Father. She's a vet, and someone had brought it into her surgery with a hurt wing, probably done by a car. "Your father needs something to look after," she told us.

We would rather it had been us.

Walt Whitman was the name Aunt Joe had given the owl. It was a big bird, a pale barn owl, about a foot high, large as a cat, with a fawn-colored back and skull feathers ending in a sort of widow's peak over its eyes. The rest of its feathers, front, face, and underwings, were snowy white. The eyes were huge, black, and staring. I suppose it was a handsome beast, really, but we hated it. We felt it had supplanted us. There was something spooky and startling about its habits—you never knew where you would come across it suddenly, in the airing cupboard, or staring at you from the top of a bookshelf, or the handlebars of Helen's bike, or the kitchen dresser, or the oven. The oven and the medicine cupboard were two of its favorite spots.

"It's not hygienic!" Helen stormed at Father, but he said, "Rubbish. Owls are very clean creatures. And Whitman has completely cleared this house of mice. There isn't one in the place nowadays."

That was true. Mice had been a problem before. You do get them in old houses.

Whitman spent a lot of time in Father's study, perched on top of a bust of the poet Edgar Allan Poe.

And because of this, Father insisted that we always knocked before going into the study—"So as not to startle Whitman."

"Really I bet it's to give Father time to look as if he's been working," Helen muttered.

But Father insisted that the owl *helped* him to work; its soundless presence in the room was an aid to concentration, he explained. I remembered that he used to say the same thing of Ma. "The only person in the world whose being in the room didn't prevent me from thinking," he had said about her, and sometimes he called her "My gracious Silence."

The owl affected our life in a good many ways. The landing window had to stay wide open at all times, rain or fine, hot or cold (and at Christmas it was *very* cold) for Whitman's comings and goings. The TV had to be turned off at ten sharp because, Father said, Whitman didn't care for the noise and vibration. Our friends with dogs were severely discouraged from coming to the house; in fact our friends were discouraged altogether; Whitman, said Father, didn't care for a lot of laughter and voices, or thumps and pop music, or smells of sausages and fries cooking. Whitman didn't like Helen practicing the cello, according to Father, and he simply hated the sound of my trumpet.

"That bloody owl's just an excuse not to have us in the house at all!" Helen burst out one evening, close to furious tears because Father wouldn't let us give a party.

"Helen! I will not be spoken to like that! In any case I don't know how you can have the heart even to think of giving a party so soon after Marian—" His voice dried up and he sat staring at Helen with what seemed like hate.

"Don't you see, you silly man, it's because we want to

take our minds *off*? How can we do that, when we have to tiptoe about all the time as if the place was an—an intensive care unit?" And then Helen rushed out of the kitchen and up to her room, slamming doors all the way.

And Whitman, disturbed, left his perch on the plate rack and ghosted about the house on great pale wings as if blown by an invisible gale.

Father simply stared at the calendar, obviously willing the last week of the holidays to go by at double-quick speed.

When we came home at Easter it was the same, only worse. Whitman was plainly fixed with us for life. Father had formed the habit of buying him little delicacies at the pet shop: foreign mice and lizards, things like that. The owl was more relaxed in our house; he made more noise than he had at Christmas, suddenly let out a weird shriek every now and then, which could startle you almost out of your wits. Or he would do a kind of loud snore, also very disconcerting, or suddenly snap his beak together with a loud click. He was not a restful housemate. Despite this increase in vocal activity Father had, to our discomfort, begun to address the owl as Silence. Whitman, he said, was a silly name, not suitable, not dignified. Besides, Whitman was a silly poet. Silence was much more suitable.

All the old rules and regulations were in force, and some new ones too. Transistors were totally banned, so was playing table tennis. Father was afraid that Silence might get overexcited and swallow one of the balls, which could kill him.

"I wish it would," said Helen furiously. "If Father were to *marry* again, I suppose I'd hate it, but at least it would be possible to understand, and sympathize, because he's lonely and—and unfulfilled; at least that would be *natural*. But to be tyrannized over by a beastly *owl*— that's just absolutely *un*natural and spooky—it's like something out of those Poe tales that Father used to read us."

In the old days, when Ma was alive, we all used to read aloud to each other quite a lot; now we never did anymore. I daresay, if pressed, Father would have been able to come up with some reason why Whitman—Silence—wouldn't like it.

"Do you think we could kidnap Whitman?" I suggested. "Pick a time when Father's out of the house, put the beast in a basket, and take him off on our bikes to some distant spot, and leave him there?"

"We could try," said Helen.

So we tried. We rode twenty miles—to Cranfield Forest—and left Whitman on an oak stump.

He was home before we were. So that was no good.

"Owls are very place oriented," Helen said. She had been reading about them in the bird book. "They use the same nest year after year. Obviously Whitman looks on this house as his nest now. . . ."

"Well, then, I think we have to murder him."

"*Murder* him?" Helen looked aghast; but then she looked thoughtful.

For days we went around without speaking; we were all of us obsessed by the owl, one way or another. The awful thing was that he did, in some way, remind me of Ma; there was something about his pale face and widow's-peak brown cap and great dark eyes that somehow called up her face, but in a teasing, horrible, unreal way. I suppose that may have been at the bottom of his fascination for Father.

I spent hours racking my brain to think of some foolproof way to get rid of the owl. It would have to be done without the least chance of arousing Father's suspicion, or the results would be dreadful: he'd probably kick us back to school and forbid our coming home at all, send us to labor camps during vacations and never speak to us again. But really, for his welfare as much as ours, I thought the deed must be done, only how? Poison, for instance, was out of the question; anything of that kind would point to us.

One night, after thrashing about, wide awake, for hours, I got up long before dawn. I sat hunched on my wide windowsill, gazing out. Our house lay on the edge of the town and beyond our garden hedge was a big hundred-acre field of young winter wheat, beginning to grow thick and green; beyond that lay a little wood. The sun, on the right, came up into a dim red cloudy sky like a thin melon-slice of blazing gold; into this theatrical light came a buoyant flitting shape which I soon recognized as Whitman, methodically quartering the wheat field for breakfast. He flew quite silently, coasting with very little effort; then, every so often, suddenly dropped with a wild flapping of wings. I've read that a barn owl can bring back a mouse to the nest every fifteen minutes. I don't think Whitman caught as many as that; but then he had no chicks to feed. The situation was unnatural for him too. Seen flying, his body looked wedge shaped, and the wide pale wings looked almost translucent with the marmalade-colored sunlight coming through them. And then, Mother's face looking out between them, when he turned his big black eyes in my direction. . . . He has *got* to go, I thought, though at that moment I felt quite sad about it; he was so handsome, coasting to and fro in the early light that, just then, I felt a kind of sympathy with Father. All the same, he has to go, or we shall end up stark crazy.

It was at that moment I had the idea how to do it.

Father was due to go up to Edinburgh that day, to receive an honorary degree from the university. No cash in it, just bags of honor, he said rather dryly. Still, it would be beneficial for him to get away, the first time he had done so since Ma's death, and he would stay a night in Edinburgh and return the following day.

He gave us endless instructions.

"Don't forget to lock up, last thing. And make sure all the lights are out. And mind you leave the landing window open, so that Silence can fly in and out."

At least we didn't have to worry about feeding Silence; he was a pet who provided his own diet, to do him justice. Though I didn't doubt Father would bring him back some fancy titbit from Scotland, Celtic mice or Caledonian lizards. Whitman's presents at Christmas had far outnumbered ours, which consisted of an obviously last-minute chemistry set and paint box.

Father left only just in time because road works were in progress along our stretch of lane: a new water main was being laid, there were men with drills and a great excavator and a stretch of muddy trench on one side of the road, and a long lumpy ridge where the completed ditch had been filled in. The sound of the digger and the pneumatic drills had been steadily coming closer for the past three days; Whitman hated it, and so did Father; he was really delighted to get away to Edinburgh, and particularly today, when the work would be right outside our house. In fact if he had delayed his departure by another ten minutes the men would have dug their trench right across our garage entrance and he would have had to make his journey by bus and train.

We never kissed each other for greetings or farewells anymore. "Behave yourselves," Father called, flapping his hand out of the car window, and then he drove away quickly, under the snout of the steam shovel, which was just getting itself into position.

"Where's Whitman?" I said to Helen, as we put away the breakfast dishes.

"In the pantry. Why?"

"I've had the perfect idea. Come on: we'll do it now, and then we'll go out for the day. Take a picnic to Bardley Down. The house is going to be unbearable all day, anyway, with that row outside."

We found Whitman dozing on the pantry top shelf. He did that most of the day, sometimes snoring, as I have said.

By now he was quite used to us, and only snarled and grunted a bit as I picked him up and sat him in the gas oven, on the lowest rack, having taken out the others. Then I shut the door and turned on the gas.

After that, feeling like murderers—as we were—we grabbed some cheese and apples, locked front and back doors, and fled from the place.

"There won't be any sign of how he died," I said. "Father can't possibly guess. He'll probably think Whitman died of old age. After all, we have no idea how old he is."

"Father will be horribly upset," Helen said wretchedly.

"Maybe that will be good for him."

"Just so long as he doesn't go and get another owl. . . ."

We had a ghastly day. It was cold and cloudy, not quite raining, but raw; we had brought along books in our packs, but it was too cold to stop and read them, so we walked and walked, in a huge circle, and ate our lunch standing, in a big yew forest where the trees gave us a bit of shelter, leaning against one of the big reddish trunks. At one point we heard the unmistakable screech of an owl—yik, yik! in the gloom.

"Whitman would have liked it here," Helen said sadly.

"It's no use, Nell. You know he'd only have come boomeranging back. We did try. . . ."

At last, more dead than alive, we limped home ourselves, just as dark was beginning to fall.

We had planned what to do: open doors and windows to let the gas escape, then retreat to the greenhouse for twenty minutes. The greenhouse was kept at an even temperature by an oil heater; it was the first time we had been warm all day.

"The gas ought to have dispersed by now," I said finally.

So we went cautiously indoors and flung open lots more windows. I turned off the gas and opened the oven door just a crack. I didn't look inside the oven. Hadn't the heart. Thought I'd wait till morning.

"I'm going up to bed," I said. "Don't feel like supper."

"Me too. Is it safe to go to sleep, though?"

"Open your bedroom window wide. And don't go striking any matches."

We crept to bed. I had expected to lie awake, racked by guilt and horror at the deed we had done. But I didn't; I slept as if I had been karate-chopped.

It was Helen who lay awake. When she came down in the morning I was alarmed: she was whiter than Whitman's shirtfront.

"Ned! *Whitman has been haunting me all night!*" she croaked. "He's been perched on my bed rail!"

"Oh, come on!" I said. But I was pretty scared myself —not of ghosts; I thought Helen was having some kind of breakdown. She looked so white and wild and trembling that I wondered if I ought to call the doctor.

"He made me think of Mother!" Helen wept. "Oh, Ned—why in the world did we do it?"

Just then Whitman—or his ghost—came coasting into the room on silent wings.

"Keep him away—keep him off me!" Helen shrieked.

Whitman made for the oven—the door of which stood open. And that made me realize for the first time that there was *no corpse inside.*

"It's all right, you dope—he's *not dead.*"

At that moment there came a peal at the front door.

"Gas inspector," said the man who stood there. "I've come to reconnect you and check."

"Reconnect—?"

"Didn't you know? The excavator cut the gas main yesterday. All this row of houses were cut off. Hey, what the blooming—?"

He had suddenly come face to face with Whitman, sitting in the oven.

"Oh, that's our owl," I said, weak and idiotic with relief. "He, he likes sitting there."

"Pretty stupid, dangerous place to let him sit," said the gas man. "Unless you fancy roast owl."

And he went about his business of reconnecting and testing.

That day we stayed at home. Our spirit was broken. We endured the hideous row made by the excavator and the drills—a few yards farther along, now; we did our school vacation work and washed some clothes; I mowed the lawn, Helen made a shepherd's pie against Father's return. That meant turning Whitman out of the oven. Restless and displeased, he found himself a new perch on the front hall coatrack. I suppose being shut inside the oven had insulated him nicely, the day before, from the noise of the drills and the thuds of the steam shovel.

"I hope they don't cut the gas main again," said Helen. "I'm dying for a bath."

At teatime, Father came home. Cross and tired, he flung open the front door—and Whitman flew out, straight into the jaws of the excavator. One crunch, and he was done for . . .

Father and Helen wept in one another's arms.

"He was so like Mother," she sobbed. "He had just her way of looking at you and not saying anything—"

"Yes, yes, I know, I know—"

Father didn't blame us. How could he? The death of Silence was nobody's fault.

But of course we feel just as guilty as if we had really murdered him. After all, we meant to; it was pure chance that our intentions came to nothing. We really are murderers.

Helen seems to have washed away her guilt in tears, and in looking after Father. But I haven't: I suppose because the gas oven was my idea. And I suppose it is because of that guilt that Whitman haunts me and not Helen.

Night after night, there he is, perched on my bedrail, silent, motionless, staring at me with Mother's eyes. Whether I'm at school or at home, it makes no difference. Nobody else sees him.

Strangely enough, I'm starting to grow rather fond of him.

The King
of Nowhere

The alarm clock whirred through the dark and
Mado, still tired after a noisy and disturbed night,
stretched out a hasty hand to silence it. With eyes tight
shut, she rolled out of bed, stood up, shuffled her feet
into slippers (they all slept in trousers and sweater, those
days), and moved off like a robot to the kitchen. It was
freezing cold and tidy. They had a rule among them,
firmly kept, that, because of probable night distur-
bances, the kitchen must be left orderly as a ship's
bridge by whichever one of them was at home during
the evening. The blackout blind was still pulled down, so
Mado was able to switch on the light. Plus one, she
thought to herself. She had a game of pluses and minuses
for beginning the day. If the mail arrived before she left
for work, if Matt came home, if she saw a cat on the way
to the office . . .

A kettle stood ready filled; she lit the gas (another
plus) walked along to the bathroom, washed and
brushed her teeth (water in the taps; yet another plus)
then returned to the kitchen, made tea, and let it draw
while she took cups, milk, sugar, from the cupboard;

then she carried the tray, yawning, into the living room where her younger brother slept on a divan.

The blackout was still in place there too. She switched on the table lamp, lit the gas fire, and turned on the radio, which sighed out a sad little nasal minor-key tune, *"Lazybones,"* theme song of a morning music program.

"La-azy-bones—sleepin' in the sun—How you spec' to get your day's work done—?"

Tom rolled over in bed, cocooning himself, resolutely turning his back on morning or tea or his sister.

"Come on, wake up!" she said. "You know you've got to. Anyway, it's Friday. Weekend tomorrow—"

"And when you—go fishin'—I bet you—keep wishin', The fish won't grab at your line—"

Tom gradually turned over, uneasily, hostile, still subhuman, but reached out a skinny arm, took his cup of tea, and began drinking it. Mado sprawled, relaxed, in her armchair, the fire puttered and purred gently, and presently an announcer gave them the war news.

After it was over, Mado cautiously undid the curtains, letting in a dim, frosty morning light.

"Come on now, get up, dormouse boy," she said. "I'm going to start breakfast. Dried-egg fritters on fried bread. I expect Matt will be home quite soon."

Her expectations of this were not so high as her voice suggested but, in fact, while she was mixing the dried egg powder to a thin paste with milk and flour, Matt, their elder brother, came in from night shift and sat on the kitchen table while she supplied him with tea and toast.

"No trouble here?" he said. "We spent half the night in Fleet Street putting out incendiaries."

"None very close." Mado sat down and bit into a piece of toast. "One fairly big one a few blocks north—in Marchmont Street, perhaps."

Tom came in wearing pyjamas and sweater, face red from scrubbing, hair up in damp spikes.

" 'Lo, Matt. Where's mine? Isn't it dark? Hellish cold too. We don't seem to get daylight anymore. I'll be late tonight—sixth-form debating society."

"You're supposed to be *dressed* for breakfast." His sister handed him a plate of fritters.

"I *am* dressed." His tone was injured. He bolted the greasy food, washing it down with copious draughts of tea. "Is there another cup? Any marmalade left?"

"You finished it yourself."

"When does the new period start?"

"Monday."

"Oh, heck!" Morosely, he scraped a little brown sugar over his toast.

"And go easy with the marge."

"All right, all right!" Dumping his plate in the sink, he stomped out.

"Betty rang up," said Mado to Matt. "Asked how much longer you'd be on the night shift. I said you'd ring her back."

"She wants me to take her to a film."

"What's wrong with that?" asked Mado, surprised at his tone. "I thought you liked her?"

"Oh . . . too tired in the evenings. Rather come back here and listen to records. How's Andy? He okay?"

"Seems quite serene."

"Bombs begun to worry him?"

"No; I don't suppose they will. Why should they?"

"*I* dunno. Any more tea? Thanks. I'm off to bed. I'm

going out at five; lecture on gas, effects of. But I'll be back by eight."

"Good. So will I. That means I needn't wash the dishes this morning. Tell Tom to hurry as you go past—he'll be late for school."

Mado dressed herself in office clothes and scanned the groceries cupboard. Then, as Matt had come out of the bathroom, she did her hair in front of its mirror and put on makeup.

Tom had clattered down the stairs already, swinging his school bag, shouting good-bye over his shoulder. Mado left Matt slumping down onto the divan, and, bracing herself, went out into the winter day, which was windless but raw, icebound, and misty. Although her office was only ten minutes' walk from the flat she had twice to make detours to avoid bomb damage. Wooden barricades were placed across streets, men were digging with picks and pneumatic drills; the air resounded with the clink of iron on stone. The building in which she worked had windows broken, and trees in the square outside it were shattered and splintered. As usual, Mado spent the first half hour of the working day sweeping grit and broken glass from the gray and battered parquet floor.

As she walked home in the dusk across Bloomsbury Square carrying a bundle of reports to read at home (nobody tried to work much after four, the office lights were too dim and flickering) Mado encountered her sister Joyce—tall, beautifully dressed, high heels, with a poodle on a long lead. Joyce must know someone who's just come from Cairo or New York, Mado reflected without malice, observing her sister's silk stockings.

"Hullo, Joyce. Doesn't he feel the cold, trimmed as short as that?"

"Mado. How extraordinary to run into you."

Joyce glanced distastefully at Mado's string bag, containing celery, a lump of butcher's offal wrapped in bloody newspaper, candles, bread, a bag of washing soda, and a tin of dried milk.

"Of course he doesn't feel the cold," she said impatiently. "He's used to it. How are the boys?"

"Okay. Tom passed his middle-grade piano. Matt's on night shift."

"Tom ought to be in the country. Walter says—"

"I know, I know. Safe from bombs and in the nice fresh air. But you couldn't get him away from Lenkovic."

"Piano lessons! Someone could teach him in the country."

"It wouldn't be Lenkovic, though, would it?"

"It's unhealthy, you living in that dark flat with the boys. Walter says—"

"No darker than anywhere else. It's dark nearly all the time anyway."

"It's time you were married. Here you are, almost thirty."

"Twenty-six," said Mado under her breath.

"And Nigel twenty-eight—"

"He's got his dud lung to worry about."

"Walter says—"

"Let Walter worry about the destabilization of the currency rather than our trifling concerns. Who is there to marry, anyway?"

"It must be lonely for you in the evenings," asserted

Joyce, reining in the poodle, who wanted to investigate under a bush.

"One or two of us are mostly in. And there is always Andy."

"Who's Andy?" asked Joyce sharply.

"The lodger."

"*Lodger,* where do you put a *lodger*?"

"He sleeps during the day . . . in the living room."

"Drawing room," said Joyce automatically. An air-raid siren began to sound—a long, lugubrious, rising-and-falling wail. "Oh, *blast* it." She glanced at her diamond wristwatch. "Now I'm going to be late and I'm supposed to be meeting Tim Susskind at the Savoy—I suppose there won't be a taxi for love nor money—I'll never make it—"

"No."

"*Good*-bye—" Joyce pronounced this word *Coo*-bahy, an upper-class affectation acquired at the finishing school which had conducted her into the right circles to meet, and subsequently marry, Sir Walter Prescott-Smith. Her accent, and particularly the use of this word, was a source of mildly satirical amusement to her siblings.

" 'Bye, Joyce. Be seeing you!"

Joyce hurried off, waving her arm energetically at a possible taxi, the poodle yapping hysterically alongside, while Mado walked home smiling, swinging her string bag.

Indoors, it was already dark. She turned on the kitchen light, hastily pulled down the blackout blind, put away her shopping, and began washing the breakfast dishes.

"Who is it?" said a voice.

"Hullo, Andy. It's me, Mado. How are things?"

"All right." Mado imagined him sitting on the table, as Matt had. "Are the others coming in?"

"Tom will be coming in by and by. He has some sixth-form thing. Matt's at a lecture."

"Good day at the office?"

"So-so. My secretary had had a bomb and went home early, so I had most of her work to do. Did you have a good day?"

"I went down to look at the Braques at the Tate. And then took in a lunchtime concert at the National Gallery."

"Good program?"

"I find it hard to concentrate nowadays. Unless something is really outstanding I find my mind beginning to drift back in this direction. Worried about you three, maybe. It's quite a wrench to keep away. But the Braques were worth seeing. I like his green."

"Greener than any grass," Mado agreed.

"Then I looked at paintings by war artists. Dreadful, all blood and munitions. I could do better myself."

"I'm sure you could," she said affectionately. "Why don't you try?"

"Through a medium?"

"Through two mediums, I suppose," she said laughing. "Ah, here's Tom. I'm going to take a bath. But then I want to do lots of ironing—it's nice to have someone to chat to—don't go away—"

In the bath—hot water, this day was coming up to ten plus—she thought lazily about Joyce. Unhealthy, what nonsense. How would Joyce, she wondered, react to Andy? Badly, no doubt.

Later, when she was ironing, she said to Andy, "My

elder sister Joyce thinks that Matt and I ought to get married."

"Why don't you?"

"Haven't seen the person I could fancy. Or he hasn't seen me. He's probably off at the war, whoever he is."

"I wouldn't mind marrying you," Andy said thoughtfully.

"Thank you! But you probably wouldn't have when you were—were in your prime. In the days when you knew Topsy."

"Ah, no. My taste then was for something blond and giggly."

Tom was practicing Bach two-part inventions in the next room. "He is improving all the time," said Andy. "He must have an excellent teacher."

"I know. That's why—ah, here's Matt, that's good. My pie will be done in five minutes. Andy, be a love and tell Tom he must stop playing and lay the table for supper."

The siren had just gone, and as Matt came in, they heard the mumble of German bombers overhead. Matt was carrying an ugly fat black cat.

"Good grief!" said his sister. "Where did you pick *her* up?"

"On the stairs. This is no time for her to be out. Her kittens would all have birthmarks."

"Well, she can stay the night, but she must leave in the morning. Yes, it's you I'm talking to! In the meantime you can answer to the name of Martha. And I suppose you'll want a bit of pie. One square centimeter of Spam."

After the meal, Mado read her reports, Matt and Tom played chess, with Andy sometimes suggesting

143

moves for Tom. The black cat settled down by the fire.
At one point she stuck out her chin, ecstatically purring,
and they heard Andy's chuckle.

"Are you scratching her chin?"

"She seems to think so."

"I ran into old Coo-bah," Mado said, mending a pair
of socks.

"What was she doing?"

"Getting a taxi to the Savoy. She thinks Tom should
be evacuated."

"Just let her try."

Presently Matt had to go off to work. By now the
night was punctuated by the steady buzz and drone of
the bombers, crackle of antiaircraft fire, and the regular
concussion of bombs falling, but not very near.

"Sounds like the docks again," said Mado. "But do
take care, Matt."

"No worry unless there's one with your name written. . . . Coo-bah, then."

"*Coo*-bah," they said.

"I ought to go to bed," Mado remarked, after he had
gone. But, in spite of that, she stayed on, and the three
remaining sat in friendly silence, in the dim warm room.

A week later, the sisters chanced to meet
again, standing in a line for shoes, in Knightsbridge, at
half past eight in the morning.

London was like that in those days, acquaintances
kept meeting in odd places.

"Good heavens, Joyce, I'd never have expected to
see you up so early."

Joyce looked disgusted with her surroundings.

"My hairdresser told me Abbotts were getting in some red casuals."

"My pharmacist told *me*."

"Wonder what time they'll open." Joyce shrank deeper into her mink as the line stood patiently, half visible in the icy fog.

"Half past nine, perhaps. . . . Where's your dog?"

"Left him with our cleaning woman."

"Lucky to have one. I suppose you wouldn't like a cat?"

"Certainly not! Specially any cat from you. Has fleas, probably."

"Almost certainly. But a nice nature. Andy and Tom are fond of her."

"Who *is* this Andy you keep referring to?" said Joyce alertly.

"I told you. Our lodger. Our ghost."

"Ghost?"

In the murky, frosty light of daybreak the whole line of hopeful shoe-seekers resembled a procession of gray and dripping ghosts. Joyce directed a baleful glare at her younger sister, whose hair was wound in a roll on a piece of string, and who wore a navy duffel-coat spangled with dewdrops.

"How can you talk such balderdash? How do you mean, ghost?"

"Well, he is a ghost," said Mado reasonably. "He used to live in the house, back in the nineties, before it was made into flats. He was a poet, a failure. Wrote one rather quotable piece that's in books of Victorian verse —'If I were King of Nowhere, and you were Queen of Time,' it begins. You must know it. But he knew he was a failure and in the end he gassed himself. Oddly enough,

he was a friend of our great-aunt Topsy—knew her quite
well, he says—that ought to make him a suitable friend
for us, in *your* book—"

"Will you *please* stop talking such utter nonsense!"
hissed Joyce, looking nervously up and down the damp
and patient line, as if she expected them to fall on her
sister and lynch her. "It's not at all funny and I'm not in
the mood for fantasy. *What would Nanny say?*"

Mado waited a moment before replying, and then
said gently, "Nanny's dead, as you may recall."

"It's high time you moved out of that place. What an
atmosphere for Tom to grow up in. Walter says—"

"Tom seems happy enough. We're all marking time,
really, aren't we?" Mado added mildly. "Oh, look, they
are starting to open the shop."

But it turned out that there were only shoes enough
for twenty customers. The woman in front of Joyce got
the last pair.

Thursday was Matt's evening off, so it happened that they were all in the flat together when the
land mine demolished it, reducing the whole building to
a heap of smoking rubble.

Wardens and rescue workers got there too late to
save the people buried underneath. But a cat escaped,
mewing sadly, and an auxiliary fireman, plying his stir-
rup pump on the dying flames, heard a man's voice
calling, "Mado? Matt? Tom? You three? Where are
you?"

"*Who's that?* Someone alive in there?" said the AFS
man sharply.

But there was no reply, except for a faint murmur of
"*Coo*-bahy."

Aunt Susan

All their friends said, and thought as well, that the young Caraways were a delightful couple: simple, unpretentious, easy to please, fond of all kinds of fun, happy in their uncomplicated lives. Not intellectual, not snobbish, not avant-garde, not reactionary—there was really nothing at all wrong with the Caraways. They lived in a charming Queen Anne cottage on the edge of Pinchester, a delightful country town; Delia taught in the local primary school, but the pair had not been married very long, and everyone felt it was only a matter of time before a few even younger Caraways were born, and then Delia, so home loving, so maternal, so natural, would certainly give up her job and devote herself to her children.

Simon Caraway had been an insurance agent, and quite good at it, but just for fun he had written a thriller and shown it to a friend who had connections with a publishing house; the manuscript was read, approved, published, and did most creditably; so now Simon found himself launched on a comfortable and lucrative career producing a suspense novel every nine months. To friends who exclaimed in amazement, "Where *do* you get your ideas? How in the world do you think up those awful plots in such a peaceful little spot as Pinchester?" he pointed out that all he required to do was to read the national and local press every day, where headlines such as AMUSEMENT PARK "DUMMY" PROVES TO BE CORPSE OF SHOT MAN, EX-TEACHER JAILED FOR DRUG-RUN-NING, GYPSY CURSE WORRIES LOCAL COUNCIL, ROBOT RUNS AMOK IN LAB, KILLS 5, WIDOWER INSTALLS CLOSED-CIRCUIT LINE TO WIFE'S TOMB, WIFE SUC-CEEDS AT FIFTH ATTEMPT TO POISON HUSBAND kept him amply supplied with ideas for plots.

So, year after year, Simon's books continued to ap-pear in their black-and-honey-colored jackets; "the new Simon Caraway" was always in demand at every library, and, although not affluent, the couple lived very com-fortably, since their tastes were far from expensive. Delia did all the housework and cooking herself, Simon grew, in their half acre of garden, nearly all the vegeta-bles they consumed, for he made a practice of writing only in the morning hours, devoting afternoons to exer-cise, and so keeping his health and youthful appearance.

Life went on with them pleasantly and tranquilly until the death of Uncle Paul Palliser. Paul and Susan Palliser had taken care of Delia when she was a child, her own parents having perished untimely in a motor accident, so it was natural for her to say to Simon, "Poor dear Aunt Susan, I can't bear to think of her living alone, she's such a sociable person. Would you mind terribly, Simon, if I invited her to come and live with us? There *is* the whole top floor."

There was. For the expected little Caraways had, somehow, never materialized. Delia and Simon kept meaning to convert the space to a self-contained flat, and rent it to a teacher or student from the local college of education; but somehow they had never got round to the operation.

It was equally natural for good-natured Simon to reply, "Poor old Aunt Susan, she must be feeling terribly at a loose end. She used to do everything for old Paul. Of course, darling, go ahead and invite her if you want to. Heaven knows there's room for a whole army of aunts up on the top floor."

So Aunt Susan was invited; and piled all her worldly goods into a van, and came; and within a fortnight was so settled into the life of Pinchester that it was hard to remember she had not always been there. She was exceedingly fond of the young couple downstairs, and touchingly anxious to make herself useful to them; she offered to cat-sit (since there was no baby); she offered to help with the housework, she offered to share in the gardening, she wanted to be a functioning member of the household in every possible way; the only hindrance to this was that the young Caraways were so self-sufficient already. However, Aunt Susan had her own resources; she made petit point and she was a corresponding member of several psychological societies, and found some local clubs of a similar nature to join; she attended lectures, gave them herself, and seemed happy and occupied enough.

But after a while Simon Caraway, though he wouldn't dream of finding fault with his wife's aunt, who was as well meaning as she could possibly be—but just the same he could find it in his heart to wish that she would not explain his own mental processes to him quite so often. If he broke the handle off a cup, she would say,

"Ah, that was a protest, because Delia set a small teacup for you, and you subconsciously wanted a *large* cup of tea." If he bruised himself chopping kindling, or pulled a muscle while digging, or suffered one of the other minor injuries to which all gardeners are liable, she would say, "Aha! That's because you wanted a pretext for not coming to the town council meeting with Delia and me, but wanted to stay comfortably at home and watch the Western on TV." If he forgot something, she could always supply a reason for his absentmindedness, generally a discreditable one; and if he employed logic in countering her suggestions, she said that his logic only masked and rationalized some deep-down unacknowledged atavistic motive.

Simon bore with all this good-temperedly enough until Aunt Susan started in on his thrillers. She had not read any of them before coming to live with her niece; she was not in the habit of reading much fiction at all, and certainly none in the blood-and-thunder genre; but she was a conscientious and well-mannered person; she felt that, since she was now living under his roof, it was incumbent upon her to make herself familiar with her nephew-in-law's work, so she purchased half a dozen of his paperbacks, took them to bed with her one night, and worked her way doggedly through them.

Since she had read nothing of this nature before, they had an extremely drastic effect on her; from that day she regarded Simon with a new eye.

"I'm afraid, Simon dear, that you have some terribly deep unresolved conflicts inside you," was her inaugural statement.

"I'm quite sure you're wrong, Aunt Susan," he blithely replied. "Or, if I have, my subconscious has managed to keep them awfully well concealed from me up till now. I'm really very happy and satisfied with my life, you know! I love Delia, I love this house and town, I love the garden, I make a good living—I haven't a care in the world."

"If only you could get at that subterranean layer of turbulence," she sighed. "Really, it's *terrifying*—the evidence of it is so apparent in your writing."

"So," he pointed out, "aren't I lucky? For it's extremely lucrative. *The Curse on Clapham Common* has just sold to an American book club for thirty thousand dollars, and *The Deadly Dummy* is going into a third printing, and they are negotiating for film rights of *Telex to the Tomb*."

"I'm afraid you don't have any conception of just how serious, how terribly dangerous, this may be. I *wish* you would go to an analyst, Simon—just to indulge me, just to set my mind at rest."

"But—dear Aunt—just suppose he analyzed all my deep subconscious conflicts out of me—then how would I earn a living? I don't suppose that I'd be able to get back into the insurance business now—and I'd hate to have to live on Delia's earnings."

"Well," sighed Aunt Susan, "perhaps—if you did something *really* creative for at least part of the time— for you can hardly say that writing those bloodcurdling little books is a suitable activity for a full-grown, adult human being; and if you were to give up writing—even for a few months—that might straighten you out and make a tremendous difference."

"Well," he said thoughtfully, "I daresay I *could* leave off writing for a few months—*The Curse* is doing uncommonly well—and a few months without earning might make a useful tax-loss—but what kind of creative activity did you have in mind, Aunt Susan?"

Handweaving was what Aunt Susan had in mind, it appeared; in no time at all she had a large loom installed in the dining room, all the furniture was squeezed into one corner, Simon was receiving instruction from one of Aunt Susan's new acquaintances, a neighboring lady who was a weaving enthusiast; and so, for several months, each day after breakfast, instead of going to rattle away at the typewriter in his study, Simon would go, instead, to what was now known as the loom room, and the clonk and thud of the shuttle could be heard instead, and sometimes Simon's muttered curses, when his warp and woof got into some particularly intractable tangle. He did not take naturally to the weaver's craft; and the rugs and lengths of tapestry which he produced were uniformly hideous; but he was a kindly fellow and saw that his compliance gave both his wife and her aunt considerable gratification; so he persevered.

But this success did not, curiously enough, satisfy Aunt Susan; although he had exchanged writing for weaving, Simon remained essentially the same bland, easygoing, unassailable character, and she felt that her remedy had proved merely cosmetic; the real deep-down problem was still untouched. So she now extended her campaign to include his gardening activities.

"There's something very *obsessional,* don't you think, about the way you mow and mow that lawn?" she said to Simon.

"The grass grows uncommonly fast in June," he pointed out.

"Ah, but don't you *see,* my dear boy, the motives go much deeper than you realize. All that cutting—clipping—pruning—hoeing—slashing—chopping that you do—can't you see what it is really aimed at?"

"The garden," said Simon.

"The garden is only a symbol. Can't you grasp that concept? Don't you see whom the garden really represents?"

"No, I can't say that I do."

"Your mother!" said Aunt Susan triumphantly. "All this violence inflicted on the garden is really the manifestation of profound feelings of hostility (and consequent guilt) toward your mother."

"But she's dead."

"That makes no difference. That only makes it more complicated, because she isn't there in person, and you have to take it out on the garden. Just look how short you cut those borders!"

"That was so I wouldn't have to do them again for ten days."

"No, Simon dear, you were really attacking your mother, because when you were a child she used to wash your face and scold you and make you finish the fat on your meat and go to bed when you'd rather stay up."

"Actually," said Simon, thinking it over, "I was pretty fond of my ma. She was a great one for larks—we used to have a lot of good times when I was a boy."

"Ah! That's what you *think*! But deep down—buried —almost forgotten—you will find there are all kinds of other memories—of struggles, and anger, and rage, and hatred. Now what you must do is stop gardening for a few months and try—really try *hard*—to recall all those unresolved conflicts. You will be truly surprised at what a difference it will make!"

"Oh, yes, darling, *do* try!" said Delia, who was beginning to be won round to Aunt Susan's point of view, since she heard it morning, noon, and night.

So for two months Simon stopped his gardening activities, and merely sat in the greenhouse, trying to remember forgotten quarrels with his mother.

The first result of this was that the garden became overgrown with enormous weeds. But Simon manfully ignored them, wrestling with his obdurate subconscious, which continued to refuse to yield any memories of familial conflict. What it did produce, instead, night after night, were a number of remarkably vivid dreams, which he would relate at breakfast.

"I dreamed that I saw you drowning again, Aunt Susan. This time it wasn't in the sea, but in a huge jar of golden syrup. The syrup had just reached your chin when I woke up."

"That's excellent—extremely satisfactory," Aunt Susan responded with great cordiality. "You are really beginning to cooperate. The dream shows a repressed wish to murder Delia; all husbands wish to murder their wives at some point in the marriage."

"Oh? Then why should I dream that it is *you* who are drowning?"

"You see, you are using me as a substitute figure. The subconscious always prefers to conceal its real impulses."

By now August had come, and Simon suggested a picnic by the sea.

Unfortunately, while Simon and Aunt Susan were dozing after the picnic lunch, Delia, who adored bathing, swam an injudicious distance out to sea, was seized by cramps, and drowned before she could be rescued. Everybody knew what a devoted couple the young Caraways had been; the deepest sympathy was expressed by the coroner and all Simon's friends.

But Aunt Susan said, "I'm afraid, Simon dear, that poor Delia must have absorbed *too deeply* the knowledge of your subconscious wish to drown her. I am not saying that she deliberately committed suicide—dear Delia was too strong, too brave, a character to do such a thing as that—but the awareness of your feelings *must* have contributed to her mental and physical state. Those cramps will have been a psychosomatic response to that knowledge. It is something that you will just have to learn to live with, I am afraid."

"No," said Simon, "for once you are wrong, Aunt Susan."

"How do you mean, my dear boy? You cannot seriously be suggesting that Delia killed herself?"

"No indeed I am not. I put two tablespoonfuls of powdered glass into her hard-boiled egg sandwich. That was what gave her the cramps."

"*Simon!* You must be joking! You can't mean what you say?"

"No, I am perfectly serious," said Simon. "I began to see that, if your theories were correct, drowning Delia would appear to be the only solution to my problem."

"*What?!!!*"

"The only difficulty," he went on, "is that now I find drowning Delia was evidently *not* the solution."

"What do you mean?" Aunt Susan asked with chattering teeth.

"Why, because of my dreams! I still keep dreaming about *your* death, Aunt Susan. Only now the death has changed its form. I keep dreaming that you are being smothered in a handwoven rug. And what," inquired

Simon, picking up a large hideous handwoven rug
which he had recently completed, and advancing on his
wife's aunt in a decidedly menacing manner, "what do
you suggest that I should do about that, Aunt Susan?"

Find Me

After the funeral Prince Tom managed to escape from his attendants and slip away. This was not hard, for he was small, and everybody was crying, they had handkerchiefs to their eyes and did not see him go.

A footman had once told him about the house in Kettle Street, where you go when you have lost something. The house is old, and empty, probably haunted. It has been empty for years. In one of the bedrooms is a mirror, and if you are brave enough to go upstairs and look in that mirror, you will see the thing you lost, lying in the place where you lost it.

Tom thought he was brave enough. He felt so sad that he did not think *anything* could frighten him.

Kettle Street lay a long way off, in a poor run-down part of the city, miles from the palace. Nobody paid any heed to Prince Tom, hurrying, head down, in his black coat, sometimes studying a street map he held in his hand.

Number Thirteen Kettle Street was a tall, shabby house, no different from its neighbors, with blank windows and broken steps leading to a scabbed and peeling door.

Tom tried the handle. Suppose it was locked? But, no, it was not. He opened the door and walked in, closing the door again gently behind him, waiting a moment, for it was dusky inside, with his heart going bang-bang-bang among his ribs.

Then he started up the stairs he saw straight ahead. The stairs did not feel at all safe: they creaked and sank as he made his careful way. At the top were three doors. He chose the middle one, but that led to a room with a great hole in the floor, so he tried the right-hand one. There was the mirror! tilted on a stand, throwing an oblong of silver light across the dirty ceiling.

Tom stole across to the mirror, avoiding holes and rotten spots in the floorboards. All his mind was on what he had lost, as he gazed down at the slanted glass.

Part of the mirror surface was worn away, and, under the glass, there were black patches. But, as Tom gazed, he found that he could see a long distance, as if through a telescope. Rooms he could see, and houses, streets, and gardens; they slid and blurred and moved on, changing all the time, but all familiar, places where Tom had lived and played, eaten and slept. And in all those places were things he had lost. Oh! he thought. There's that spotted wooden dog!—it must have fallen into the pool—and my red scarf—and the little book Nan gave me—

Better not think about Nan. If he had not lost his lucky piece of string, perhaps Nan would not have caught pneumonia and died.

There was the string! Caught, with a grubby handkerchief, under a root of the big walnut tree in the palace garden.

If only he had known before. . . . Drawing a deep shaky breath, rubbing his nose on his sleeve, Tom turned to go. What a lot of things I've lost, he thought. Suppose an old, old person, Nan, for instance, came? Why, it would take weeks to find all the lost things! He paused for a last look in the mirror, to thank it, perhaps. The glass was calm now, nothing in it. But yes, there was! Another face, a girl's, thin, rather sad, older than Tom, almost grown up—but nothing like so old as Nan had been. Stepping forward, she gave Tom a little nod, then studied the glass.

"You lost something too?" he whispered.

"My job," she whispered back. "The factory closed. . . ."

Leaving her to her search, Tom went downstairs. But he sat down abruptly on the bottom step. Inside, he felt as if something had snapped, a long, long thread.

After all, Nan had looked after him ever since he was born.

He laid his head down on his knees.

By and by, steps came down behind him. Tom stood, and looked at the girl. At first her shape slid about, blurred, like the pictures in the mirror. Then it steadied.

"Did you find what you were looking for?" he asked.

"I—think so. Did you?"

"My string? Yes. Now I know where it is."

"Then," she said, "hadn't we better get you home, so you can find it?"

And she took his hand in hers, where it fitted comfortably.

Give Yourself
a Fright

The two Matheson brothers always, whenever they met, began to argue and dispute. Never, from nursery days on, had they agreed about anything. The argument would begin over a trifle, then become more and more rancorous. As boys they soon fell to hitting, kicking, and biting; as men, grown calmer and more sensible, they merely turned their backs on one another and went their different ways. Evan, the elder, became a parson; no better, no worse, you might say, than plenty of others who esteem themselves competent to lay down rules for their neighbors; Ralph, the younger, was clever at his books, passed various examinations, and so became a professor.

For ten years, or it might be more, the brothers had kept apart, until Ralph, returning from travel overseas, had the misfortune to be laid low by a putrid fever and, after weeks of illness, was so enfeebled that his physician forbade him to resume his teaching until he had spent at least a month's convalescence in a peaceful neighborhood, preferably near the sea.

Wondering where he might go, Ralph now bethought him of his brother Evan, who had recently been appointed incumbent of a large parish on the east coast. Time and indisposition had perhaps softened past memories of brotherly disputes; Ralph wrote propitiatingly, had a friendly enough response from Evan, inviting him to spend as much time as he liked in the spacious rectory, therefore packed up his bags and his books, and took a train to the nearest rail station, Salt Ness, where his brother met him.

"Why, Ralph, boy!" exclaimed Evan, easily hoisting up the three heavy portmanteaus and tossing them into the back of the pony trap, "you don't look as ill, by far, as I had feared, my dear fellow. You look more like a prosperous little grocer than ever! Pink, shiny, and stout; I'll always think it a great shame that you didn't go into the cheese and wine business!"

Ralph reddened with annoyance, for it was true that, although he had become a scholar, and well enough respected at his college, he remained a decidedly unimpressive figure, short, inclining to obesity, with small gray eyes, shiny cheeks, and lank black hair. Whereas his brother, tall, bony, lantern faced, with fine gray thistledown locks, appeared every inch a man of God.

The visit went well enough, despite this unpromising start. Ralph, for the first few days, kept to his chamber or to the walled rectory garden, rested, and read his books and papers under the mulberry tree, while Evan the rector busied himself about his parish duties. Unexpectedly, for that part of the country, they were blessed with a spell of mild sunny autumn weather; late flowers bloomed, roses and asters; while the swallows lingered perching on telegraph wires and twittered together as if debating whether to postpone their journey south.

The brothers had never found it easy to converse, because their natures were so opposed. But—fortunately—since they last met, Evan had invented a game, and had amused himself by constructing it very completely, with its board, counters, dice, cards, small wooden men, and all the other neat little component parts; Evan had always been clever with his fingers and could draw, write, engrave, mold, or carve as well as any monk. So the two brothers spent many hours together playing this game, which was based on the book *Pilgrim's Progress* by John Bunyan. Hazards in the play included the Slough of Despond, the Valley of Humiliation, Vanity Fair, Doubting Castle, and the Valley of the Shadow of Death. The men on the board comprised Christian, Giant Despair, Mr. Standfast, and the Foul Fiend Apollyon. There were also Hobgoblins, Satyrs, and Dragons of the Pit, besides a Man with a Muckrake and people with burning faces.

The game was an intricate and exciting one, and the two men managed to forget their half-buried animosity in the duel of wits with which it presented them. They were well matched, for though Ralph's was the better intellect, Evan possessed a shrewd, keen readiness to guess and grasp at a possibility and put it to use. Ralph was the first person to whom he had shown the game, and Evan felt kindly toward him for grasping its workings so well and appreciating its niceties. Ralph, indeed, admired the ingenuity of the game very much, and told his brother that he ought to take out a patent on it and sell it to some stationery company or toy manufacturer; he might well make his fortune from it. Evan, however, replied quietly that he had no wish to make his fortune; life in this quiet seaside spot and the care of his parishioners gave him all that he required. And Ralph was aware that he had been delicately reproved.

Sometimes, after playing at the Pilgrim's Progress game for several hours, the brothers would fall into conversation about the nature of good and evil. Oddly (considering their former antipathies) these talks did not end in bad feelings or angry words, although their views were wholly opposed. Possibly because they had been pitting their wits against one another in play, they felt the less need to fall out in earnest.

"Evil is a negative," said Ralph. "Evil of itself has no reality. It is merely the absence of good."

"You are entirely wrong," replied his brother mildly. "Evil is a positive and terrible force. It is Satan, against whom we have to be continually on the watch."

"Fiddlesticks!" returned Ralph smiling. "Brother, dear brother, you are a hundred years behind the times! The character of Satan is an outworn concept. In your game here—ah, yes!" He looked at the tiny figure of Apollyon with his claws and outspread wings. "In your *game*— but not in reality."

Evan glanced at his timepiece. The two men were sitting at the stone table under the mulberry tree. Evening light shone through the tree's branches. Now the evenings were growing shorter and chillier; in a sudden puff of cool wind, every now and then, winter's approaching breath could be felt.

"I have to pay a call on a parishioner," said Evan, without making any direct reply to Ralph's last remark. "Would you care to come with me?"

"By all means," answered Ralph, secretly gratified at this invitation; his brother had not previously made any such suggestion, but had simply taken himself off at regular intervals on his parochial duties. Today was a Friday and it was a few minutes before five o'clock; Ralph had noticed with what regularity Evan always left the house at this time; to attend a parish meeting, he had thought.

Ralph picked up the walking stick which he used as an aid to his somewhat slow and halting progress, and prepared to accompany his brother.

The two men set out, not, to Ralph's surprise, along the village road, but in the opposite direction, toward a solitary steading that lay below a headland, at the end of a long, wandering lane.

"Who lives in such a remote spot?" asked Ralph, as they approached a small, shabby cottage which stood half hidden behind elderly apple trees.

"A man called Penfold—Amos Penfold." Evan opened the half-rotted gate and made his way along a moss-covered brick path.

From the somewhat neglected habitation—though the garden was well enough tended and the orchard trees, he noticed, were covered with healthy fruit—Ralph had surmised that some aged, palsied hermit, far gone in years, must live here; he was surprised when the door was opened by a tall, burly man with a broad, tanned face and a thick crop of dust-colored curls. The high-colored face of Amos Penfold seemed meant for good nature, but his wide mouth was tucked back tightly at the corners and his pale eyes were watchful and wary. He made no acknowledgment of Ralph's friendly smile, merely jerked his head, silently inviting the gentleman to walk inside if he wished, and at once addressed himself to the rector.

"Sir, you an't come a moment too soon. I can feel

him growing restless. I can feel him strain to be free, and to come out."

"Now, my good friend, remember what I have told you so many times; calm yourself," answered the rector, walking into the cottage as one well accustomed to be there, and throwing his hat on the deal table. "He is powerless against our prayer, you know that well. You and I together are stronger than he is, with the might of our great Defender behind us and His mercy as a shield before us. So fling those traitorous fears out of your heart. Your Father in heaven has you in His hand and will not let you fall."

"Ay, sir, that's as may be," said Amos Penfold doubtfully, "but 'im, that other one, was my master first, and well he knows it. And I get black downhearted, times, and that's the truth."

"Now, Amos, banish those thoughts, and kneel down beside me, and pray," ordered Evan firmly.

Ralph, no believer, was somewhat taken aback when the two men knelt without ceremony upon the not particularly clean brick floor, and the rector put up a long and powerful prayer "for the strength and defense of our brother Amos Penfold against the powers of darkness and the temptations of the pit." Amos Penfold shut his eyes and clenched his fists, sweating with the intensity of his feelings, as if he were visibly, physically engaged, then and there, in a life-and-death battle against some actual adversary.

Ralph, not a little embarrassed by such a scene, removed his hat and stood holding it awkwardly in his hand, wishing he had never come into the untidy kitchen. The cottage struck him as very doleful; it seemed damp, uncared for, and smelled of stewed tea and boiled potatoes.

After a while, since his brother had embarked on yet another lengthy prayer, he retreated softly, on tiptoe, through the front door, which he had left open, deciding to pass the time in exploration of the outside regions.

The garden was a more cheerful place than the house; there were currant and gooseberry bushes, cabbages in neat rows, and, all around, the apple trees weighed down by fruit almost ready to be picked. Many of the apples looked too small for eating, and round at the end of the cottage Ralph discovered the reason for this: a huge old cider-press, embedded in a stone foundation and operated by a giant screw. Ralph wondered if it was still operated; the screw appeared well oiled and in working order; the tank, set in front to collect the juices, had recently been scrubbed. People in the village must still make and drink home-brewed cider.

The sound of footsteps in the lane attracted Ralph's notice and he saw, over the hawthorn hedge, a small peaky boy, who, noticing him, stood hesitant by the front gate. Ralph recognized the boy as Barney Voles, a protégé of the rector's, or at least a fairly regular visitor to the rectory. He was a sad, skinny child whose father had perished in a farming accident and whose mother did cleaning work at a few houses about the village. Barney, passing through the rectory garden on errands to the back door, had several times been greatly attracted by the Pilgrim's Progress game and had stood by the stone table, breathing audibly through his mouth and giving off a rather stronger smell than Ralph cared for, of unwashed boy and dirt-impregnated clothing. Sometimes he offered advice.

"Watch out for your man on that square, Reverind—the hobgoblin'll get 'im!"

"Ah, thank you, Barney." And the rector would carefully shift his piece out of harm's way.

"Hadn't you oughter take those two outa the Slough, Mister Ralph?"

"No, I am choosing to leave them there, Barney. Sometimes you have to lose a smaller piece in order to save a greater one."

"But that ain't fair on *them*!" The boy's face would crumple with distress.

"Run along to the kitchen, Barney. Mrs. Pickthorn will give you a slice of bread and jam."

Obediently, but casting backward glances, the boy would retreat, followed by a lean tortoiseshell-and-white cat which seemed to accompany him everywhere. The cat was here, now, in the cottage garden, attentively, from its perch on a pile of bricks, watching something that moved in the hedge.

"Why, Barney," remarked Ralph in slight surprise, "what are you doing here, so far from home?"

"Me mum sent me on an errand. She sent a pudding for Uncle Amos." He showed a basin wrapped in a cloth.

"I see. Well, I believe you had better wait a minute or two. The rector is in the house just now—ah—talking to Mr. Penfold."

"I knows that." The boy nodded. "Mum on'y let me come down 'ere Fridays—arter the reverind's been a-talking to Uncle Amos, settin' 'im right for the week. Other times, I ain't allowed."

Slightly perplexed by this, Ralph was about to question the boy further when Evan and Mr. Penfold came out of the cottage.

167

Amos was thanking the rector with fervent and evidently heartfelt gratitude.

"I thanks Your Reverince more than I can say. That oughta keep 'im at arm's length for another sennight. The comfort you brings me, sir, is better nor anything in this wide world. Ah, Barney, is that you with my Friday pudden?"

Penfold received the offering with a kind word, but the rector frowned at Barney. "How often have I told you, Barney, that you are not to come down here?"

"But if me mum send me, sir?" Barney whined.

"Well, tell your mother that I do not at all approve. Let her find some other messenger—or let Mr. Penfold fetch his own pudding. Do you understand me?"

"Yessir."

Sniveling, the boy trotted off, with his cat careering behind. Evan shook his head, looking after the pair, then turned to his brother.

"Ralph, I brought you here so that Mr. Penfold can tell you what it is that troubles his mind."

Greatly embarrassed by this direct approach, Ralph mumbled something about "not wishing Mr. Penfold to divulge any private matter that he might, on another occasion—" but Amos Penfold, calmed and restored, apparently, by the ritual indoors, explained simply, "You see, sir, 'tis the Evil One who stands there a-waiting for me."

Like many men who lead solitary lives, he made frequent gestures while he was speaking, as if to help his words, which came slowly; now he made a motion of the hand which might have referred to the shed at the end of the cottage containing the cider press.

"The Evil One," Ralph responded rather blankly.

"Yessir. Ever since I were a young lad I seen him a-waiting."

"You can see him? With your eyes?"

"Outa the corner of me eye, like, sir. Not there"—he pointed ahead—"but over *that* away, just where I can't see him so plain."

"But you can tell me what he looks like?"

Amos Penfold gave a shudder.

"Not so's I could really picture him to you, sir. Acos I on'y see him sidelong, you understand? He's a bit hunched up, kind of a gray shadow, with points of light for eyes, very very bright; and he's all tattered and torn; that's acos he be so old, you see, sir."

"Old, yes; I suppose he is very old," Ralph replied, humoringly.

"He be always a-waiting; he's a-waiting there *now*, you know—a-listening to every word we say. And one day he'll get me—I know it."

"Come, come, come, Amos, this is foolish talk, and you know that it is," reproved the rector somewhat sharply. "He will *not* get you; I have told you that over and over. You have done nothing to give him power over you. Nor will you!"

"But *he* knows that I will, sir!" wailed Amos lamentably. "He knows that, one o' these days, I'll maybe do what Uncle Giles did to me. And then he'll have me, he'll have me by the soul."

Ending these words on a long, miserable howl, Amos Penfold bolted back inside his house and slammed the door. Nor could all the rector's angry rattlings and remonstrances persuade him to reopen it.

"I'll see ye next week, Reverind! But don't-ee desert me—don't-ee do that, indeed!"

"I regret, now, that I invited you to come down and meet him," Evan said as the two men walked back along the lane. "I never thought it would affect him so."

"But I found his obsession highly interesting," argued Ralph. "What did his uncle Giles do to him?"

"He has never told me. He was an orphan, brought up by this uncle, who, I have gathered, used him with atrocious cruelty and himself came to an untimely end. Amos himself is completely mild and gentle, has never, so far as I know, hurt a living creature in the whole of his life."

"It would be better if he had," pronounced Ralph.

"Are you clean out of your wits, my dear fellow?" demanded the rector, turning to stare at his brother.

"Not at all! This kind of obsession with sin is mostly to be found in those who have never committed more than the most trivial fault. What they need is a kind of inoculation—a taste of wickedness, just one taste. That way, you see, what you do is give yourself a fright—scare yourself away from the real thing, probably forever."

"You are talking dangerous nonsense! You do not know what you are saying!"

"Speak for yourself!" sharply retorted Ralph. "Dangerous, indeed! And how about the danger of keeping that poor maniac on the loose, a hazard to himself and the whole community, just because you fancy yourself as a saintly man of healing? How's that for overweening pride and vanity—hey? What the man Penfold needs is a doctor. Not to be lectured by you once a week."

Then Ralph stopped abruptly. Dammit, he said to himself, I've done just what I swore not to, snapped at Evan. And we had been getting on so well. And it's the last week of my visit—why couldn't I have kept my stupid mouth shut? In seven days more I'd have been gone, deuce knows when we'll ever see each other again; what a fool I am to be sure.

Evan, however, seemed resolved not to take any further offense. He walked for a considerable distance in silence, until they reached the Voles cottage, on the outskirts of the village. Here he knocked, put his head round the door, and said, "Mrs. Voles, I have warned you before, and I do so again; it is not safe or sensible, it is asking for trouble, to send the boy down to Amos Penfold's house."

A thin whining angry voice came out, like a snake's tail shaken from a cloth.

"Oo else can I send, Reverind, answer me that? I've not got all day to go running errands down the lane! Some folks never thinks on other folks' troubles."

Evan rejoined his brother with a red spot of annoyance burning on either cheek.

But all he said was "She is a most ill-conditioned woman. I am glad to do what I can for poor Barney. It is hard for him, having no father. . . ."

That evening was chill and gloomy, with a faint brume in the air which raised goose pimples as it touched the skin; the two men were obliged to eat their meal indoors; and the rectory was not a comfortable house; its downstairs rooms were cavernous and cold, furnished cheaply with ugly Victorian pieces which, on account of their bulk, were not wanted elsewhere.

Ralph, feeling tired and out of sorts, was glad to go to bed early. In the night his rest was disturbed by singularly unpleasant dreams; most of these, fortunately, dissolved and left no memory behind after his awakening, but one stayed with him: it concerned the cider press at

Penfold's cottage, which he saw in process of being used to make cider, the flat press being screwed down tighter and tighter, and juice running out into the tank; but what kind of person or creature operated the machine he could not see, for it was stepping and moving about in the darkness of the shed; except that it had very long skinny arms, and its clothes appeared to be in tatters. He had the most lively wish *not* to see any more of it, and would have been glad to escape from the spot, only that he did not like to turn his back on the creature in case it suddenly ran out after him. Mercifully at this moment he woke, and lay until dawn, very unwilling to sleep again, in case the dream came back.

Next day he felt weak and indisposed, wretchedly fatigued, and some of the symptoms of his previous illness returned to him; it was a gray rainy morning and he stayed in his bedroom until noon. During the afternoon, however, a fresh breeze blew the clouds away and a brilliant sun tempted him out of doors; the two brothers sat and played their game amicably under the mulberry tree and found, as usual, that they were very evenly matched; sometimes Evan drew ahead in the score, sometimes Ralph, but neither for very long.

The boy Barney came and watched them for a time, but he seemed subdued and lachrymose, making no suggestions about their play.

"What's the matter, Barney?" asked the rector mildly. "Do you have a cold?"

"No, Your Reverince, it's my cat Tib; he've gone missing; I've called and hunted all over the village but nobody's seen him, not nowhere."

"I wouldn't worry, Barney. He's probably off hunt-

ing and will come back, by and by, with his coat full of
fleas; cats are taken with the urge to roam at times."

"Yes, sir," said Barney, but he sounded unconvinced.

The next day being Sunday, Ralph, who still felt
twinges of remorse toward his brother, decided to attend matins, which hitherto he had not done. The
church, a fine Norman building with a handsome tower,
by far too large for its present-day congregation, was
hardly a tenth filled. Ralph noticed Barney, and his
mother, a thin, tallow-faced slatternly-looking woman;
but Amos Penfold was not there. Evan preached on the
text from Matthew 16:23, *Get thee behind me, Satan.*
The word *Satan,* he said, in the Hebrew language, signi-
fied the Adversary. An adversary should never be
treated with, not any way whatsoever; have no dealings
of any kind with Satan, he urged his hearers; avert your
eyes from any glimpse of him, stop your ears against his
whispers, hold your breath against the stench of his cor-
ruption. For the slightest touch of evil may infect you
with a dread and incurable disease.

The rector spoke very strongly, and with deep con-
viction, but his audience, Ralph observed, listened in
stolid and unmoved silence; their expressionless faces
did not suggest that the subject had touched them very
greatly.

The two brothers did not play their game that day,
for Evan never indulged in such pastimes on a Sunday;
after lunch he read, or reflected, or slept, in his study.
Ralph had made no reference to the sermon at lunch; it
had, in fact, somewhat annoyed him. He could not help
feeling that it was aimed at him, an unfair tactic in a
covert game which he and his brother seemed, tacitly,
to be playing. Silence was his only rejoinder; and after

173

the meal he took himself out for a walk along the shore and up the neighboring headland.

There, for some time, he sat on a rough stone wall gazing at the sea, gray, wrinkled, and inscrutable below him. Then on the shore he saw a small, spindle-shanked figure wandering forlornly; he recognized the boy Barney and went down to join him.

"Still looking for your cat, Barney?"

"Yes, sir. Leastways I haven't found him yet." But Barney's expression lightened just a trifle; he said, "As you're with me, Mr. Ralph, would you object to go back by Uncle Amos's place? Parson don't like for me to go there on me own. But if I was with you, sir—"

"Certainly, Barney. But do you think your cat is very likely to have gone there?"

"Uncle Amos did use to give 'im a fish head sometimes, sir."

So the two crossed the beach, skirted the orchard, and returned along the lane by the disheveled cottage, where Ralph, seeing Mr. Penfold at work among his cabbages, put his head over the gate, and called, "Good afternoon, Mr. Penfold. Barney here wants to know if you have seen his cat?"

The man at work straightened and gave the two visitors a very long, strange look; a look imbued with such a chill, silent, *measuring* quality that Ralph had a feeling as if a razor-sharp knife had been dragged sideways over his flesh. He was on the point of retreat, without waiting for an answer, when Amos suddenly spoke.

"Cats are accomplices of the Evil One—along with owls, toads, bats, and such wicked vermin. I'll have no truck with any of those."

Taking this to mean that Penfold had *not* seen the

animal, Ralph hurried on, motioning the reluctant Barney to follow with a jerk of his head.

"The rector is right, Barney. You should not go near that man. There is something amiss with him. I do not think he is safe."

"But sposin' he've poor Tib shut up somewhere?" demanded Barney on a wailing note.

"That is not in the least probable. Why, after all, should he? Now you run along in to your mother."

Barney would plainly have preferred to accompany Ralph to the rectory, but Mrs. Voles had seen them through the dirty window of her cottage. She came hurrying out in her slippers, draggle haired and clamorous.

"Well, there, where have you *been*, Barney, I don't know, I'm sure, I've been *that* put about and worried, for Mrs. Pickthorn from the rectory came and just look what she found in the road—"

What Mrs. Voles held out was a paw. Barney screamed aloud at the sight of it, for it was a cat's paw, flecked white and tortoiseshell.

"I'll—I'll be leaving you with your mother, Barney," said Ralph, very much perturbed, and he made haste on to his brother's house.

"Did you hear what Mrs. Pickthorn found, Evan?" he asked.

"The cat's paw—yes, indeed—poor Barney, I fear he will be distressed. But these accidents happen to pets. Do you remember our dog Towzer, shot by the keeper . . . and the tortoise that vanished away—"

"Evan, that paw had been *flattened.* and torn out by the root."

"Run over by a farm cart, I daresay. Such things do occur. But fortunately the village is full of cats, and

175

many of them, doubtless, about to produce families of kittens. The boy can be consoled soon enough. I will ask Mrs. Pickthorn to give him a piece of plum cake next time he appears."

Filled with intense irritation against his brother, Ralph retired upstairs and endeavored to distract himself by preparing a series of lectures to be delivered when he was well enough to resume teaching.

Evan is a self-satisfied fool, he thought. I truly believe that he thinks he is directed by the hand of God, and can do no wrong. It would be salutary for him—it is what he needs—to be reminded that he himself is not faultless, that he is capable of committing an error, just like any other.

The week passed quietly enough. Barney, they heard, was sent to visit cousins in Marlinby; for several days he did not appear at the rectory. Ralph worked at his lectures; the two brothers had little to say to one another until one day Ralph made a suggestion about the Pilgrim's Progress game.

"I have been rereading the book," he said. "You have not made use of Mount Sinai and the Hill Difficulty. Why not construct a pair of little mounds—you could do so readily enough, with clay or gum arabic or plaster of Paris; you could have a hollow in Mount Sinai and a light shining from it (a birthday cake candle would serve)—for the burning fire . . . and the player who passed that way would lose ten points. Then, for the Hill Difficulty, the task would be for the player to guide his man all the way to the top of the hill without losing his roll—you remember Christian drops his halfway up the hill and has to go back for it? And that makes him late and so he has to encounter the lions in the dark? All this you have left out, my dear Evan, but I think it would enliven the game and make the appearance of the board more interesting. And maneuvering the roll up to the top of the hill would be a difficult feat—you could have a tiny ball, or piece of tube."

Ralph delivered all this speech very softly and solicitously, keeping innocent, attentive eyes on his brother; but Evan, not at all piqued, it seemed, by suggestions that his game might be improved, welcomed the ideas eagerly, and set to work that very day on the construction of a pair of hills.

"We can fasten them to the board with tiny pegs," said he, "so they may be removed when the board is folded. Why don't you, Ralph, make the lions? You have seen real lions on your travels, I daresay, and so must be much better qualified to fashion them than I would be."

But Ralph, rather peevishly, said that he had no gift for modeling lions, and would leave that kind of work to his brother.

"*You* are the handyman of us two," he said. "All I am good for is to bring forth ideas and notions out of my head. Don't you remember how, when we were young, you used to call me Ralph the Romancer?"

"So I did," agreed his brother laughing heartily. "Or Rosy Spectacles Ralph! You were always such a boy for whimsical caprices and fancies—whereas I saw the practical, necessary thing, straight ahead, and went on and did it. It is queer that now *I* am the one who has invented this game."

He spoke with considerable satisfaction.

"Yet now too," suggested Ralph softly, "*you* are the one who believes in that crouched, tattered figure of

Amos Penfold's—that fantasy creation, hiding in the corner, biding his time!"

"Indeed I do!" Evan's tone was loud and forceful. "So would you, my friend, if you had a quarter of my experience. But there—it is no use expecting a teacher, an academic, to acquire such knowledge. You have lived out of the world, removed, among your students, your books and papers—"

And you? thought Ralph, throttling back his rage. You deal out rewards and scoldings to your little flock, as you see fit; what does that tell you about the real world, about the heights and depths of evil and good?

But with an effort he held his peace, and when the model mountains were made and dry, he offered to paint them, and accomplished this task with fair skill, also fashioning a little arbor of twigs, where Christian might drop his roll, and a set of neat steps for the pilgrims to climb.

Mrs. Pickthorn the housekeeper said to Barney's mother, who came to do some scrubbing, that it was a fair wonder to see two grown men so wrapped up in a frippery game; but there, that was gentry for you, always pickling their wits in some nonsense or other. And Mrs. Voles entirely agreed.

"Barney!" she said sharply, "You come back from out there! Don't you go a-hanging round those two gentlemen, now! I've a plenty jobs for you to do at home, errands to run"—and Barney, thin, pale, and dejected, none the better, it seemed, for his visit to the cousins, came drooping away from the table under the mulberry tree, and followed his mother homeward.

Evan glanced at his watch occasionally, for the hands were moving toward the hour of his weekly visit to the man Penfold; but Ralph cunningly distracted him by suggesting a couple of highly ingenious variations and improvements on the route through the Valley of the Shadow of Death. Absorbed in the new possibilities offered by these, and new modifications which might then come into play, Evan let the time slip by without remarking it until, suddenly hearing the church clock chime the half hour, he was abruptly recalled to his self-imposed duty, and jumped to his feet with a shocked gasp.

"Merciful heaven! How can it be so late? Oh, what have I done—how *could* I—?"

And without sparing a moment to get his hat or jacket, he set off up the lane at a run.

"Don't put yourself in such a fidget!" Ralph called after him. "The fellow can manage without you for fifteen minutes, surely?" But he received no reply.

Half contemptuous, half guilty, Ralph slowly followed his brother down the lane. At the Voles cottage he saw Barney's mother peering out of her doorway. "It ain't like His Reverince to be late!" she called out in a croaking, angry tone. "If the likes of us can't depend on the likes of him, who the plague *can* we depend on?" But Ralph passed without answering her.

When he reached Penfold's cottage he began to imagine, for a thankful moment, that all was well. An unbroken silence reigned; the birds were hushed, there were no voices to be heard, nor sound of human activity, no footstep nor cough, not even the creak of a well handle nor the click of a latch.

But on the brick path from gate to front door lay a broken pudding-basin and one of Barney's shoes.

179

"Evan?" called Ralph, now hideously alarmed. "Evan—where are you?"

Not without a cold quake of fear, he walked to the open doorway and put his head inside. But the kitchen was empty; neither his brother nor Amos Penfold were to be seen. Nor the boy.

"Evan?" called Ralph again. "Mr. Penfold? Where have you got to?"

Overcoming his extreme reluctance, he returned to the brick path and, in the gathering dusk, walked on round the cottage.

As he neared it, the open-fronted building which housed the cider press appeared to contain nothing but dark. Yet, as Ralph came closer, a dim gleam of machinery could faintly be seen. The tank, low down in front of the press, had been filled with liquid, which overflowed and ran away into the weeds at the side of the path. Ralph paused, aware of a stickiness under his foot. And as he halted, looking watchfully round him, he glimpsed from the corner of his eye—the very briefest glimpse, just a flickering movement—he caught sight of something at the side of the press: a stooped, crouched figure, jerking at the handle which governed the screw. The figure turned, and for the fraction of a second, Ralph had the impression of two eyes, brilliant points of light, focused on him; then, wholly unstrung by terror, he was running back along the slimy brick path, aware of nothing but a soft, padding tread, following close behind him. . . .

LAUGH TILL YOU SCREAM!

With each and every one of these scary, creepy, delightfully, frightfully funny books, you'll be dying to go to the *Graveyard School!*

Order any or all of the books in this scary new series by **Tom B. Stone**! Just check off the titles you want, then fill out and mail the order form below.

☐	0-553-48223-8	**DON'T EAT THE MYSTERY MEAT!**	$3.50/$4.50 Can.
☐	0-553-48224-6	**THE SKELETON ON THE SKATEBOARD**	$3.50/$4.50 Can.
☐	0-553-48225-4	**THE HEADLESS BICYCLE RIDER**	$3.50/$4.50 Can.
☐	0-553-48226-2	**LITTLE PET WEREWOLF**	$3.50/$4.50 Can.
☐	0-553-48227-0	**REVENGE OF THE DINOSAURS**	$3.50/$4.50 Can.

Bantam Doubleday Dell
Books For Young Readers

BDD BOOKS FOR YOUNG READERS
2451 South Wolf Road
Des Plaines, IL 60018

Please send me the items I have checked above. I am enclosing $_____
(please add $2.50 to cover postage and handling).
Send check or money order, no cash or C.O.D.s please.

NAME _____

ADDRESS _____

CITY _____ STATE _____ ZIP _____

Please allow four to six weeks for delivery.
Prices and availability subject to change without notice.   BFYR 113 2/95